"Wanted for murder of girl in love nest . . . Charles White . . . released from Raiford Penitentiary recently . . . may be heading for Palmetto City . . . This man is armed and dangerous . . ."

The radio blared the news. I gunned the motor and hit eighty, looking back over my shoulder.

I was wanted, all right. Wanted for murder and heading straight for trouble. Headed for Palmetto City—and my wife. Armed and dangerous as hell . . .

Only I hadn't murdered yet. I hadn't killed anyone. But I might kill now—*to find the man who had!*

HUNT THE

KILLER

DAY KEENE

WILDSIDE PRESS

INTRODUCTION

"Day Keene" was the pseudonym of Gunard Hjertstedt (1904–1969), an American novelist, short story writer, and radio and television scriptwriter. Keene published around 50 novels, a long list of short stories, and served as the head writer for many radio programs, including *Little Orphan Annie* and *Kitty Keene, Inc.* Several of his novels were adapted into movies, including *Joy House* (by MGM, 1964) and *Chautauqua* (released as *The Trouble with Girls* by MGM, 1969).

Hjertstedt adopted his "Day Keene" pseudonym when he was breaking into pulp magazines as a new author. An editor told him that he loved a crime story, but couldn't possibly put a name like "Gunard Hjertstedt" on the cover. "Day Keene" was born on the spot. Hjertstedt adapted his mother's maiden name, Daisy Keene, to the more manly "Day" Keene.

—John Betancourt
Cabin John, Maryland

A DAY KEENE BIBLIOGRAPHY

Framed in Guilt (also published as *Evidence Most Blind* (1949)
Farewell to Passion (also published as *The Passion Murders* (1951)
My Flesh Is Sweet (1951)
Love Me and Die (1951)
To Kiss or Kill (1951)
Hunt the Killer (1952)
About Doctor Ferrel (1952)
Home Is the Sailor (1952)
If the Coffin Fits (1952)
Naked Fury (1952)
Wake Up to Murder (1952)
Mrs. Homicide (1953)

Strange Witness (1953)
The Big Kiss-Off (1954)
There Was a Crooked Man (1954)
Death House Doll (1954)
His Father's Wife (1954)
Homicidal Lady (1954)
Joy House (1954)
Notorious (1954)
Sleep with the Devil (1954)
Who Has Wilma Lathrop? (1955)
The Dangling Carrot (1955)
Murder on the Side (1956)
Bring Him Back Dead (1956)
It's a Sin to Kill (1958)
Passage to Samoa (1958)
Dead Dolls Don't Talk (1959)
Dead in Bed (1959)
Moran's Woman (1959)
Miami 59 (1959)
So Dead My Lovely (1959)
Take a Step to Murder (1959)
Too Black for Heaven (1959)
Too Hot to Hold (1959)
The Brimstone Bed (1960)
Chautauqua (1960)
Payola (1960)
World Without Women (with Leonard Pruyn (1960)
Seed of Doubt (1961)
Bye, Baby Bunting (1963)
LA 46 (1964)
Carnival of Death (1965)
Chicago 11 (1966)
Acapulco Gpo (1967)
Guns Along the Brazos (1967)
Southern Daughter (1967)
Live Again, Love Again (1970)
Wild Girl (1970)

CHAPTER ONE

IT WAS HOT. It was dark. The cell block smelled of men sleeping with dreams. Men without women for years. Of fear and despair and frustration. Night after night, alone. Three walls, a high window, iron bars. A hard, narrow cot—and you. With disinfectant replacing affection. A small squirrel in a big cage. Staring hot-eyed into the dark. Wanting a drink. Wanting a woman. Trying not to blow your top. Hysteria building up inside you.

Can you go down to the corner for a beer? Can you catch a mess of shrimp and go fishing? Can you pat your wife and say, "Tonight, huh, babe?"

No. You do what you're told. And like it.

I hadn't slept all night. And morning was slow in coming. I'd waited for it a long time. Four years the man had said. Four years I had done. Without any nonsense about parole or time off for good behavior.

I was washed and dressed and waiting when the rising siren blew. McKenny, the guard on the tier, paused in front of my cell on his way to pull the master switch.

"This is the big day, eh, Charlie?"

The lump in my throat was so big all I could do was nod.

Then he pulled the switch and my cell door opened for the last time and I lined up on the catwalk with the others. The guys who still had days, weeks, months, and years to do. Wishing me luck from the corners of their mouths as we marched down to breakfast. Not meaning it. Nothing personal. But hating my guts. For one reason. I was going out and they were staying.

I tried to eat, and couldn't. I was too excited. Then, too, the pock marks in the plaster of the mess hall bothered me. I knew them for what they were. I'd heard the machine guns make them. And if it hadn't been for Swede I could be dead instead of walking out. I could be with Mickey and Saltz. I could be in solitary. I could even be with Swede.

The thought cost me what little appetite I had.

5

A front-of-the-prison guard was standing in the mess hall door as we filed out. As I passed him, he asked:

"You Charlie White?"

"I am."

"Then step out of line and follow me."

I followed him down a long corridor, across the yard, and into a small room in the administration building. The clothes I'd signed for the day before were hanging on a wire hanger.

The guard said, "When you're dressed turn the things you're wearing now over to the supply clerk."

"Yes, sir."

"Then go to the warden's office."

"Yes, sir."

A sallow-faced cracker with jaundiced eyes, he lighted a cigarette and blew smoke in my face. "That is, unless you want to keep your denim as a souvenir."

I shook my head at him. "No, thank you. All I want out of this is a faint recollection."

He didn't laugh. "Then if I were you, I'd keep out of trouble."

"Yes, sir."

The sun lifted out of the Florida scrub and beat in through the window. I stripped and stood in it a minute, naked, letting the sun burn the prison stink off me. It was going to take a lot of sun. Then I put on the suit of clothes, turned my denims into the supply clerk, and walked into the warden's office.

He had my dossier on his desk. "So you're going out this morning, White?"

"Yes, sir."

"And glad to be leaving us, eh?"

It was as hot in the warden's office as it had been in my cell. Sweat trickled down my spine and tickled me. It was difficult to breathe. How much did they think a man could take? I'd done my time. I wanted out. By swallowing hard I managed to gulp out another, "Yes, sir."

The warden looked from my papers to me. "Fishing boat captain, weren't you, White?"

"Yes, sir."

"Your own boat?"

"Yes, sir."

He looked back at my papers. "Hmm. Four years. With no time off for good behavior." A touch of color crept into his fat jowls. "As a matter of fact you're lucky to be going out at all. You know that, don't you, White?"

6

I gave him the, "Yes, sir," routine again, leaning on it this time. So what could he do to me?

More color came into his face. He started to get sore, and changed his mind. "Okay. If that's the way you want it, White. You're several cuts above the average prisoner we get here. I wouldn't want to see you come back. But right now you're so stinking filled with self-pity that anything I might say wouldn't do a bit of good."

I wiped my face with the sleeve of my new coat. "Then why bother to say it?"

He laid a typed receipt, a sealed envelope, a small sheaf of bills, and some silver on the corner of his desk. "I don't intend to. If you'll sign a receipt for the one hundred and twenty-six dollars and fifty cents that is credited to your account, I'll let someone else do the talking."

That would be Father Reilly. The priest had given me the only news I'd had of Beth in four years. I knew she knew about Zo. But if Beth had filed suit for divorce, I hadn't been served with the papers.

He tucked the receipt in a corner of his blotter. I wadded the bills and the envelope into my pocket.

"Good-bye and good luck, White," the warden concluded the interview.

He pushed a buzzer on his desk and a new guard took me in tow. But we weren't headed for the chaplain's office. It was the first time I'd been in the death house. I didn't like it.

Swede was sitting on the edge of a desk in a small windowless conference room. He was barefoot, wearing nothing but pants and a skivy, looking much the same as he always had, except that his tan was gone, the lines in his face were deeper, and his eyes seemed even bluer.

"You've ten minutes, White," the guard said.

He closed and locked the door behind him. The lump in my throat almost choked me. Ten minutes wasn't long enough to even start thanking Swede for what he'd done for me. I'd have been in the attempted break up to my eyes if Swede hadn't belted me unconscious.

"*Stay out of this, kid,*" he'd bellowed. "*You've only got six months to go. With me, it's different. I've got life and ninety-nine years.*"

It hadn't been much of a riot. When I'd come to, the machine guns had stopped chattering. Mickey and Saltz were dead. And Swede had picked up the big tab for caving in a guard's head.

"Cigarette?" Swede asked.

7

I took one from the pack he offered. "Thanks."

Swede sucked hard at his own cigarette, as if with time running out on him he wanted to enjoy every puff to the maximum. I had a lot of respect for the old man. A charter boat captain who knew both the Gulf and the Caribbean like most men know the streets in the town they live in. If anyone knew the score, Swede did.

"Ten minutes," he said, "isn't long. So let me do the talking, kid. Would you say I was a Holy Joe?"

The lump in my throat let go. I laughed.

"Then keep that in mind," Swede said. "Except for our age, you and me are a lot alike, Charlie. We both love the water. We've both made a good living on and out of it. But were we content with that? No." He gestured with his cigarette.

"That's why I asked the warden if I could talk to you. A man does a lot of thinking when he gets in one of these quick fry joints. And it all boils down to this; a guy hauls in the fish he baits for and at the depth at which he fishes."

He let me think it over while he lighted a fresh cigarette from the butt of the one he was smoking.

"In the old days it was different. A man had to depend on himself. There was a lot of uncharted sea for him to sail as he saw goddam fit. But times have changed. After years of sailing by guess and by God, society has set out certain buoys and markers. You got a silver dollar, kid?"

There was one in the money the warden had given me. I gave it to Swede.

He traced the lettering on the head side with his finger. "*E Pluribus Unum*. Know what that means, Charlie?"

I said, "Something about one for all or all for one."

Swede shook his head. "Naw. It means *one out of many*. And that's you and me, Charlie. And the guard who brought you here. And the warden. And the guy's who's going to fry me tonight. We're all just one of many. And you've got to swim with the school or—well, look what's happened to me. Look what happened to you when you tried to sail on your own.

"As rackets go, you had a good one. But let's add up the score. On the debit side it cost you your wife, your boat, and got you four years in the can. On the profit side you had a few roaring good drunks in Habana, a fancy, oversexed dame and the false knowledge that you were smarter than your fellow fishing boat captains. There were no lulls in your business. You brought in a good catch every time. Okay. How much dough you got?"

8

I told him, "One hundred and twenty-six dollars and fifty cents."

Swede hooted. "For four years of your time. Hell. There are guys netting mullet out of Naples, and Palmetto City for that matter, who are making that much every night. But netting mullet is hard work. So is fishing the snapper banks. Or running a charter boat. And you and me had to be wise guys. Your wife waiting outside?"

I admitted I didn't know.

"I don't know why she should be," Swede said. "A man can starve a dame. He can get drunk and beat her every night and twice on Sunday and she'll still think he's her personal Marshall Plan in a silver champagne bucket. But only if she knows she's the only woman in his life."

He went on before I could speak.

"Sort of looks like you got a little off course, eh, Charlie?"

I hesitated, "Well—"

Swede spat his cigarette on the floor. "Naw. You still don't think so. You still aren't willing to admit you made a mistake and cut bait or fish. You're still feeling too damn sorry for yourself."

He lighted a third cigarette, his blue eyes probing my face. "I know how you feel, kid. I've got a temper, too. That's one of the reasons I'm here. But don't do it, Charlie."

Even thinking of *Señor Peso* choked me. "Don't do what?"

Swede said, "You know damn well what I'm talking about. But killing your former partner because he ran out on you when the law stepped in will only bring you back here." Swede patted the wall of the death house. "And I mean here. Building up another dividend for the stockholders of Florida Power."

I wiped the sweat tangled in the hairs on the back of my right hand with the palm of my left.

Swede sucked at his cigarette. "Look. When you came back from that mess in '45 or '46 you'd been living in a bloody tide for four years. Life meant nothing. A thousand lives meant nothing. That right?"

I said it was.

Swede got up from the desk and began to pace the floor. "Well, we had a similar tide in the Gulf while you were gone. We called it the red tide. Fish died by the tens of millions. The shores and the tide flats from Apalachee Bay to Cape Sable were heaped so high with dead fish you could smell them for ten miles inland. Everyone swore things would never be the same again."

9

"I heard about it."

"But they are." Swede's eyes were surprisingly blue and clear and unafraid. "I mean the same. The water gradually cleared. The shrimp came back to the grass flats. The fish began to spawn again. Oh, maybe not quite as many as before. But nature is gradually building back."

My throat tight, I asked him, "So what's all this got to do with me?"

Swede said, "You're in clear water again, Charlie. If you're smart you'll stay there. Get a job fishing on shares. Swab out a charter boat and bait tourists' hooks if you have to. Then when you get something to offer her, find your wife. Get down on your knees if you have to and beg her to forgive you and come home."

I said, "That sounds like good advice, Swede."

He looked at me a long minute, then snuffed his cigarette. "But you aren't going to take a damn word of it. Okay, kid. It's your funeral."

The guard opened the door. "That's it."

"I've been wasting my time," Swede complained. He walked to the door without offering to shake hands. Then he turned in the doorway and said, "I won't bother to say good-bye. As long as you feel the way you do, it's just *auf Wiedersehen*. Till we meet again. I'll try to save a quart and a brunette for you, Charlie." His smile was wry. "But I'm afraid the whiskey is going to be hotter than the dame."

CHAPTER TWO

LIFE. A FUNNY PROPOSITION. The things it does to a guy.

I walked back through the yard with the guard. Inside the administration building again, he pointed at the front door.

"Okay. You're on your own, White."

I nodded. "Thanks."

He turned into one of the doors. And I was alone in the hall, without any supervision for the first time in four years. I stood

10

looking at the front door, afraid to walk out on the stoop. Was Beth waiting, or wasn't she?

She knew I was getting out. Father Reilly had written her. So where did we go from here?

There was a cigarette machine in the hall. I bought a deck of Camels, my fingers shaking so badly I could hardly get the quarter in the slot.

And what to do about *Señor Peso?*

Señor Peso. The name sounded like a gag. But it was the only name I had. Outside of Zo's.

I leaned against the wall, waiting for my hands to stop shaking, thinking about Beth, about Zo. About the mysterious *Señor Peso.*

The big veins in my temple began to pound. It had been his voice on the phone that had started all the fireworks. If it hadn't been for a guy I'd never met, the past four years wouldn't ever have been. I'd still be operating the Beth II out of Bill's Boat Basin. He'd cost me four years in the can, my boat, and more important, Beth. And now Swede wanted me to kiss him off the record.

A trusty I knew walked down the hall on an errand. When he saw me, he said, "I thought they turned you loose this morning?"

I said, "They did."

"Then what are you hanging around for?"

What could I tell the guy? That I was afraid to walk out the door? Not physically. In my mind. Afraid of what I might do. "I'm waiting for my wife," I lied.

He sucked in his breath through his teeth. "Geez. Would I like to be waiting for my wife."

And he went on about his errand. I walked a few feet closer to the front door. Past a sort of alcove. With a sofa for visitors. And a mirror on the wall. A big mirror with beveled edges. Like the one Beth had wanted for the parlor of the old home place on the island.

I stopped and looked in the mirror. Four years hadn't changed me. I was still a big, freckled face, red-haired cracker fishing guide. One hundred and ninety pounds of beef and about two ounces of brains.

"This is Señor Peso, Captain White. How would you like to make two thousand dollars?"

That had been the first time. Over the phone. With just a trace of an Ybor City accent. The time I'd been behind in the payments on my new boat, the season three months off, and Beth sick to boot. Because of me. Because of a miscarriage.

11

How would I like to make two thousand dollars? How would I like to drop a mullet net around ten ton of pompano?

And all I had to do for the dough was meet the *Andros Ancropolis*, a converted sponge boat, eighty miles out in the Gulf, and bring in a few small, waterproofed packages that fit easily into my bait well. I didn't know what was in them. I didn't bother to ask. All I knew was that they were gone when I looked in the well the next morning. Replaced by the two thousand in cash *Señor Peso* had promised would be there.

So it was wrong. So I knew it. So Beth cried all night when I told her. It was money. Big money for me. The kind of money I'd always wanted.

Money to fix up the house. Money to live like the tourists lived. Money to buy Beth the pretties I'd always promised her she'd wear. If only she'd stop her goddamn crying.

A trip to Veracruz had followed. Then one to Pinar del Rio. I'd had my boat paid for by then. Then the trip to Habana where somehow I'd met Zo. After that I was in so deep that it hadn't mattered. I went where I was ordered to go, met whom I was told to meet, got what I was ordered to get. And brought it back to Palmetto City.

Every trip a good one. No lulls in my business. Getting in deeper and deeper with Zo. Beginning to drown my conscience in rum. A big shot. Me.

I'd only made one restriction. I'd refused to run wetbacks. And after the one proposition along that line, *Señor Peso* hadn't mentioned the subject again.

It had been a lead pipe cinch. All the boys in the Coast Guard knew me. The older officers had known my father. I'd had no trouble with clearance papers. No one had ever stopped me. Until that last time.

And that trip my bait wells had to be filthy with forty thousand dollars worth of Swiss watches and French perfumes— on which no duty had been paid.

I still hadn't met *Señor Peso*. My instructions came by phone. My money came in the mail, in cash. And, once the Coast Guard lowered the boom, he had walked out on me cold.

"And whom," the federal prosecutor in Tampa had asked, "were you running this stuff for, White?"

I told him. *"Señor Peso."*

The judge almost bust his gut from laughing. And fined me five thousand dollars. Confiscated my boat. And sent me away for four years. Away from Beth. Away from Zo.

To learn how to hate *Señor Peso*.

12

I dropped my cigarette and snuffed it with the toe of my shoe. It all depended on Beth. If Beth were waiting for me, I'd follow Swede's advice. I'd start all over again.

If Beth had decided to call it quits, the hell with everything. So I was a big dumb cracker. No guy ran out on Charlie White. I'd identify and kill *Señor Peso* if I had to call for the quart and the dame that Swede had promised to save.

I walked out the front door. It was the same sun that had shone on me in the yard. But different somehow. Hotter. Brighter.

I shaded my eyes with my hand. Beth wasn't in the parking lot. Beth had called it quits. But Zo was waiting. Zo had stuck by me.

I stood a minute just looking at her. Leaning against a canary yellow jeepster. Her head bare. Her black hair shining in the sun. Wearing a white strapless sundress that made her shoulders look like they were made of cream. The dress cut low in front. Her breasts straining against the cloth. Reminding me.

I walked over to the jeepster and Zo's voice reached out and caressed me. Stroking me where it hurt. After four years without her. Without any woman.

"Hello, honey. Am I glad to see you?" Zo lifted her lips to be kissed. "I've been waiting out here since daybreak."

Her lips clung to mine. Fiercely. Her fingers dug into my back.

I thought, *To hell with Swede. To hell with everything.* It was nice to hold her in my arms.

I said, "You shouldn't kiss strange men like that. You won't go to heaven."

Zo wrinkled her nose at me. "Who wants to go to heaven?"

I kissed her again. "You devil. You cute little she-devil!"

Zo understood. Zo knew how I felt. She cupped my face between her hands. "Right here, if we could. But they'd jug both of us, Charlie." She handed me the key to the jeepster. "Here. You drive."

I got in back of the wheel. "Where to?"

Instead of answering, Zo lighted a cigarette, sucked smoke into her lungs, then put the cigarette between my lips. "Let's get one thing straight first, Charlie?"

"What?"

"No one let you down."

I started to get out of the jeep. Zo put her hand on my arm. "I mean it. The *Señor* you-know-who couldn't afford to show at your trial. It would have jeopardized the whole set-up."

"So he threw me to the wolves."

13

Zo smiled, white-toothed. "Let's say the sharks." She dug in her purse and came up with a bank passbook. Mine. "But you haven't done too bad."

I opened the book and looked at the figures. I'd lied to Swede. I wasn't broke. I was filthy. For every month I'd spent in a cell, someone, *Señor Peso* presumably, had deposited one thousand dollars, American, to my Habana bank account. The last figure showed I had $48,546.00 on deposit.

I put the book in my pocket. "How come?"

Zo showed more of her teeth. "Perhaps I had something to do with it." Her smile faded slightly. "You are all mine now? Or do I still share you?"

I named her what she was.

Zo continued to smile. "Even so. Sluts have been known to love their man." Her Spanish accent grew more pronounced. "Even as much as a wife." She looked around the parking lot. "And I do not see any wife waiting for you."

It was hot in the parking lot. The top of the jeepster was down. The sun burned like a blow torch. I took off my coat and laid it in the back seat. And the devil climbed in with us.

I thought, *The hell with Beth. She didn't even care enough to show. To hell with everything. To hell with trying to kill Señor Peso. It wasn't his fault I was caught. And in his way the guy has tried to play square with me. Forty-eight thousand bucks is a fortune.*

I tilted Zo's chin and kissed her.

Suspicious, she asked, "Why?"

I said, "I'm sorry I called you that name. But my nerves are shot." I jerked my head at the pile of stone. "A few more months in that joint and I'd have gone over the blue wall."

Zo smiled through a mist of tears. She called me by her pet name. "You are nice, Captain Charlie. I like you. And now shall we go?"

I eased the jeepster out of the lot. "You tell me where."

Zo said, "Straight across the state. To Cross City. I've engaged a cabin on Dead Man's Bay. Just us for two or three days. Then one of the boys will put in and take us on to Habana. That all right with you?"

After four years in a cell? The sky and palm trees, the pound of surf on the beach, and Zo. "You kidding me?" I asked her.

Swede had been wrong. Wrong about a lot of things.

Zo sat closer to me on the seat. "You still like me a little bit."

"I like you a lot."

"Only like?"

14

"Well, love then."

She sat even closer to me. "You thought of me once in a while?"

"A thousand times."

"In a nice way?"

"No."

My answer seemed to please her. "I'm glad." She was breathing hard, her breasts rising and falling with each breath.

"Why should you be glad about that?"

The devil leaned over the seat and lighted twin candles in her eyes. "Because I am not a nice girl. Being nice would bore me very much, I think."

She was all Cuban now. The two words came out, "I theenk."

I laughed at her.

She was hurt. "Why are you laughing at me?"

I said, "Because you're cute."

"As cute as Beth?"

I fought a sick feeling in my stomach. "Don't mention her goddamn name."

Zo smiled like the bitch she was. "Whatever you say, my darling. You would like a drink perhaps?"

"I would."

She took a fifth of Bacardi rum from a paper bag, uncorked it, and handed it to me. I let it trickle down my throat like wine. Perhaps a half a pint before I handed it back. She put it on the seat beside her.

After being away from the stuff so long it hit me almost as hard as Zo's kisses. There was little or no traffic on the road. I let the rum spread through my body until my nerve ends were tingling. Then on a lonely stretch of highway I pulled the jeepster off the road onto a grassy spot and in under a clump of palmettos.

Zo made no protest as I took her in my arms. She didn't call it 'foolishness' as Beth might have done. Sweat was trickling down her cheeks, staining her dress, under her arm pits, across her stomach. From an inner fire.

"I hoped you would, darling," she panted. "Four years is a long time."

I said, "You're kidding me."

"No," she protested. "I'm not."

Cupping my face in her hands, she plastered her lips to mine. I touched her and caught on fire. And after that we had no need for words.

15

CHAPTER THREE

IT WAS LATE AFTERNOON when we reached the cabin. On the shore of Dead Man's Bay. We'd stopped three more times. Once to eat. Once to pick up more rum. In Gainesville and Cross City. And once along the road.

Both of us were fairly high. Zo filled with plans for the future. Me satisfied with the status quo. Zo, a bottle, a cabin. What more could any man want after four years in a cell?

The cabin, when we reached it, was a pleasant blur in a stand of slash pine on an isolated white beach that looked as if a careful housekeeper had swept it. A rutted sand road led back from the Highway to the Gulf. As nearly as I could tell, the nearest house, and that a fishing shack, was over a mile away.

The Gulf looked the same as it always had. Blue and darkly mysterious in the brief afterglow of the sun. Stretching out to hell and gone. To Yucatan. And through the channel to the Caribbean.

It looked good to me.

Zo understood. "You like?"

"I like," I admitted.

She unlocked the door of the cabin. A two room shack with a combination living room and kitchen and a bedroom. "Then why don't you go for a swim, sweetheart? While I put on some coffee and get us some supper."

Between the rum and emotion she'd gone all Cuban now and supper came out *suppair*.

I put the groceries we'd bought in Cross City on a table. It was a good idea. After four years away from it, the rum was hitting me hard. If I wanted to stay with the party I had to lay off the stuff for a while.

I said, "Swell," and peeled off my clothes where I stood, Zo laughing like mad but fending me off when I tried to get amorous.

"Later, sweetheart."

16

I left her to the coffee and padded down to the water bare-footed. I swam out until the shore line was a blur in the deepening dusk. Then I turned on my back and floated, looking up at the first faint stars. Thinking how much I'd missed them. How much I'd missed the water. Yes, and how much I'd missed Zo. Almost glad Beth hadn't met me. Thinking how different mistresses were from wives. It was marriage without restrictions. Zo never cried when I got drunk. Zo got drunk with me. Zo always wanted to do whatever I wanted to do, whenever I wanted to do it. Zo didn't give a damn what people thought. So I'd been in jail, I was out. And that was the end of it. More, Swede had been wrong about the location of her heart. Sure she liked me that way. But if her affection hadn't been deeper than that, she wouldn't have shown up at the prison with the forty-eight grand. And turned it over to me. When a dame like Zo loved a guy, she stuck.

I turned over and swam back to shore slowly, leaving a phosphorescent wake. Hungry for Zo again. Normally now. Without any immediate need. So I was a heel. So I'd been born fifty years too late. So I should have lived before society set up the buoys and markers that Swede had yapped about. What the hell? I couldn't turn back the clock. All I could do was live.

I stood a moment on the beach, squeegeeing water from my body with my hands, looking out to sea, sucking in the salt air, imagining being out there on the water again. In a Diesel powered fifty-footer. Or a sloop-rigged ketch. Or even a kicker-powered rowboat. Any damn thing that would float.

Then I walked back along the path to the cabin.

Zo had lighted two lamps. One in the kitchen. One in the bedroom. I followed the yellow carpet into the kitchen. There was coffee water boiling on the battered old kerosene stove. And a pot of black-eyed peas. And a heavy iron spider put to heat for the big steak we'd bought in Cross City.

"You have fun?" Zo called from the bedroom.

"It was swell," I called back.

There was an opened bottle of rum on the table. I took a swig from the neck of the bottle. Then started into the next room to see what Zo was doing and I tripped over the clothes I'd dropped and damn near broke my neck.

Zo heard me laughing and asked what was so funny.

Still sprawled on the floor I laughed, "Your housekeeping. Why didn't you hang up my clothes?"

I could imagine her slim shoulders shrugging. "How do I know but what you *like* to hang your clothes on the floor?"

17

She'd been hitting the bottle while I swam and her chicken and yellow rice accent was even more pronounced. "And when I am a little girl my mother told me. 'Zo, always remember this. To please a man you should always let him do what he likes.' You like?"

Still sitting on the floor, I whooped, "You bet I like."

Then I picked up the bills and the crumpled envelope that had fallen out of my coat when I'd kicked it. The envelope was the one the warden had given me, along with what money I'd had coming. With my name typed on the front. Along with my number.

Charles A. White, 34408133.

It was probably a song and dance about keeping my nose clean in the future. Or a religious tract. I started to throw it away. Into the trash box by the stove. Then remembered that since the riot all incoming mail had been retyped.

I ripped it open. Two tens and a five dollar bill fell out. All the good from my swim gone, my skin suddenly felt cold and clammy, I got to my feet and held the letter under the lamplight. It read in Beth's precise phrasing—

My Dear Charles:

If it were at all possible I would be waiting for you when you have finished your penal term. Unfortunately, one of us has to work. So, as a substitute, since you are probably without funds, I am enclosing twenty-five dollars for train fare.

If you are sober when you reach Palmetto City, ready to settle down and be the type of man I thought I married, I will be glad to discuss the matter with you.

All my love,

Beth

Then, as an afterthought, she'd added:

P. S. We will start all over.

It was the type of letter Beth would write. She'd been a school teacher when I married her. And her family had looked down their noses when she'd married a charter boat captain. Who didn't go to church. Who drank. Who lived in a run-down old mansion on an island.

But Beth loved me. She'd sent me train fare to come to her. She was ready to start all over. And here I was—all mixed up with Zo again.

18

Zo called from the bedroom. "What is the matter, Captain Charlie?" She added a liquid love phrase in Spanish. "I thought we had an appointment while the coffee water was boiling."

I took another drink of rum and tried to do some straight thinking. I'd promised Beth it was for always. I loved her. She loved me. And with Beth and her slim blonde beauty out of my life forever, nothing would ever be quite right again. The money, the excitement. Zo, were just poor substitutes for what I really wanted. Beth to love me. Love me like Zo loved me. To the point where nothing else mattered.

Maybe with forty-eight grand she would. I could build her a nice house. In a nice section of Palmetto City. Get a job she approved of. Maybe in a store. Maybe selling real estate. Be the type of man she wanted.

Zo called again. "Is something the matter, honey?"

I told her the truth. "Yeah. Plenty."

I padded into the bedroom carrying the letter and the bottle of rum.

Her hair a black frame against the white of the propped up pillow, Zo was lying on the bed smoking a cigarette.

"Now what?"

I sat down on the bed beside her, wishing she weren't so lovely, wishing I'd never met her.

"Now what?" she repeated.

I said, "So I'm a heel. I'm sorry. But you and I are washed up. As of now. I'm going back to Palmetto City and my wife."

Zo laughed. "You are kidding." She reached out a hand to caress me. "You are having a joke with me. No?"

I shook my head. "No."

Zo withdrew her hand. "But why?"

I handed her the letter from Beth. She read it, the hand holding her cigarette resting on her concave stomach. White smoke curling up like incense rising in front of an idol. A very lovely idol.

Finished, she looked at me. "This is a *love* letter?"

I said, "It's just Beth's way of writing."

For some reason I was embarrassed for Beth. She could have been more demonstrative. Not that she ever had been.

Zo looked at the letter again. "Where did you get this?"

I said, "The warden gave it to me. It's been in my pocket all the time. But I didn't open it until now."

The letter seemed to fascinate Zo. She read it through again. "After four years she writes you this. After four years without you, she is willing to *discuss* the matter?"

19

I made more excuses for Beth. "Beth isn't a tramp. Going to bed with a man means something to her."

"Bah." Zo dropped the letter on the floor. "This woman with whom I used to share you does not love you, Captain Charlie." Crimson fingernails bit into my forearm. Zo's voice was as fierce as her eyes. "I am a woman. I know." She raised her left palm breast high. As if she were taking an oath. "And I would have been at that gate this morning to offer myself to you if to raise the fare to get there I had to sleep with every man between here and Habana." Hot tears filled her eyes. She shook them away. "It would have meant nothing to me. Your love would have made me clean again. Pleasing you would have been all that mattered."

I slapped her. Hard. "Stop talking like a slut."

Her eyes turned sullen. She wiped her cheeks with the back of her hand. "Why should I? You seem to think I am one."

I tried to explain how I felt, and couldn't. I was all twisted up inside.

"Have I asked for any money from you?"

"No," I admitted. "You haven't."

Zo lighted a cigarette from the butt of the one she was smoking, reminding me of Swede. As if time were running out on her, too. "Let's have a drink," she suggested.

I handed her the bottle. She sipped a drink from the neck and handed it back to me. I wet my lips and put it on the floor by the bed.

Calmer now, Zo said, "Be reasonable, sweetheart. How much could you possibly make commercial fishing or running a charter boat?"

"I could do something else."

"What?"

"Sell real estate."

"I laugh."

I got a little sore. "Even so. I'm going back to Palmetto City. Now. Tonight. And get a job. And make Beth proud of me. And remodel the old house. Or buy a new one. And raise five or six red-headed kids. And be disgustingly honest."

Zo took my hand. "I could have children for you."

"Little bastards."

"Would that make you love them less? If they were your children?"

"No."

Zo moved my hand a few inches. "Love me."

I cursed her. "You devil. You black-eyed devil."

20

"But cute?"

"But cute," I admitted.

Then she was in my arms again, her body straining against mine, chanting, "I love you, I love you, I love you."

Beth, the letter, nothing, mattered for the time being. Nothing at all.

It went on for what seemed like hours. Then Zo's eyes suddenly went wide. The corners of her lips turned down. I thought in passion. She opened her mouth and screamed.

"No! Please, God!"

Her fingers left my hair and spread across the back of my head as if trying to protect it.

I thought she was screaming at me. She wasn't. The blow came from one side and behind me, crashing through her fingers to my head.

Zo screamed again. In pain now. I turned my head in time to see a blur of white face through the fog of unconsciousness that was reaching up to engulf me. A faceless face. A face like a man with removed cataracts might see without his glasses. A shapeless, featureless face, topped by a blob of dark hair.

Then the leaded butt of the gaff hook the killer was using as a club landed a second time. And still clinging to Zo, I floated out into a sea of space. On a red flood tide.

As if from a great distance away, Zo whispered, "I love you, Captain Charlie."

Then the flood tide swept us out to sea, turning, twisting, buffeted by huge waves. Then just as we passed the last buoy marking the channel of consciousness, I thought I heard the flat slap of a pistol. And Zo's body relaxed in my arms.

CHAPTER FOUR

I CAME TO lying face down in a tangle of wet seaweed, wondering why it was so dark, and where I was.

I tried to lift my head. I couldn't. The pain was too intense. Then one by one the shattered pieces of reality began to fall in place. Like the curlicues of some monstrous jigsaw puzzle.

21

I was in a two room cabin on Dead Man's Bay. With the oil lamp in the bedroom turned out. The wet seaweed was Zo's hair. The yielding substance was her body. Still soft but cold now. Her passion spent for all time.

I lifted my face from her hair, rolled to the far side of the bed and was sick. Between the bed and the wall.

I'd read the letter from Beth. I'd told Zo I was through, that I was going back to Palmetto City. I'd taken Zo in my arms. For the last time. Then what had happened?

Then Zo had cried out, "No. Please, God."

But it hadn't been God who had slugged me. Rolling back across Zo's cold legs I felt on the floor for the bottle of rum. The rum tasted good. It washed the taste of Zo's hair from my mouth. I took a second drink, then forced myself to feel through the dark until I found her heart. There was no beat. Zo was dead, had been dead as long as I'd been unconscious.

I felt through the dark for the lamp. It was still intact, still on the table beside the bed. With a package of book matches beside it. I struck a match. Then sitting on the side of the bed I lifted the chimney of the lamp and lighted it.

A yellow glow spread through the room as I replaced the chimney. A moth attracted by the flame batted its body against the glass. The drone of mosquitoes outside the screened window grew louder.

All I could see of Zo, without turning, was one white arm and hand. Dangling over the edge of the bed. Her fingers barely touching the bloody handle of the gaff hook with which I had been slugged.

I picked up the gaff and weighed it in one hand. The handle was loaded with lead. Whoever had slugged me had meant to kill me.

But why?

I took another drink of rum, studying the pattern of the rag rug. I had no illusions concerning Zo. I'd met her in a Habana night club. She was in the rackets up to her eyes. And, for all she had sweet-talked me, I doubted she had remained physically true during the four years I'd been in prison. For one thing she had to eat. A jealous boy friend was the obvious answer. One of my successors had slugged me and killed her. But how had he known where we were?

A flight of mosquitoes found their way through a hole in the screen and settled on my bare back. The ticking of a clock annoyed me. I looked up and around the room and saw a battered alarm clock on the dresser. I had been out for hours. It had been seven when we reached the cabin. Now, if the clock were right, it was five minutes of twelve.

Still without looking at Zo I carried the lamp and the bottle into the kitchen. It smelled of burned peas and hot metal. The black eyed peas were a charred mess in the pan. The coffee pot had long since boiled dry. The heavy iron spider glowed red.

I turned off the burners of the stove and set the lamp and the bottle on the table beside the groceries we'd bought in Cross City. My clothes were still lying on the floor. Where I had dropped them to go swimming. I walked to the screen door and looked out. The clearing lay snuggled in the hot Florida night. The Gulf lay placid in the moonlight, a silver streak stretching to Yucatan. The canary yellow jeepster was still parked under a slash pine. There lay the Gulf of Mexico. There lay the road to the highway. A lump formed in my throat. But I wasn't going anywhere. After sixteen hours of freedom, I'd been.

I picked up the lamp again and walked back into the bedroom. Zo was lying on her back, her eyes open and staring at the rain-streaked beaver-board ceiling, a small, puckered, brown hole in her left temple.

I sat on the bed beside her and picked up her dangling hand. All four fingers on it were broken. Had been broken when she'd tried to protect me by cupping her hands on the back of my head. I looked at her left hand. It was the same as the right. Zo's hands had taken the full force of the blow. If it hadn't been for Zo, I'd be dead.

I sat holding the lamp, looking around the room. It might have been a stage set for a movie. A chair was tipped over just so. A torn shade dangled in the window. A shattered rum bottle drained of its contents lay on the rag rug.

"I'm sorry, Zo," I told her.

Then I walked back in the other room and picked my coat from the floor. It was heavier than it had been. An automatic pistol, undoubtedly the one with which Zo had been killed, sagged the right hand pocket. I put the gun back in my pocket, dropped the coat back on the floor, and put on my shorts and socks. Then I put on my pants and shoes. And had another drink.

I could see the scene as the newspapers would describe it. A recently released ex-convict and his girl had rented an isolated cabin to celebrate his release. A drunken brawl had followed. Zo had clubbed me with the gaff. And I had shot her.

I put a cigarette in my mouth and struck a match. But I forgot to inhale. My cigarette still unlighted, the match burned down and burned my fingers. Without me feeling it.

23

The lump in my throat choked me. This was murder. And I was tagged. I couldn't prove that I hadn't killed Zo. All the evidence was against me.

A half dozen prison guards had seen me get into the yellow jeepster. The waitress in Gainesville who'd served us a meal would identify me as the man who had been with Zo. The liquor store man in Cross City would testify that he had seen us together and I had been drinking heavily. So would the grocery clerk.

No one would believe my story. My money was still in my pocket. Zo hadn't been attacked. I couldn't describe the faceless man I'd seen. He was as vague as my testimony concerning *Señor Peso*. There was no known reason for him to have done what he had.

I thought of what I'd told Zo:

"Even so. I'm going back to Palmetto City. Now. Tonight. And get a job. Make Beth proud of me. And remodel the old house. Or buy a new one. Raise five or six red-headed kids. And be disgustingly honest."

That was a laugh.

What breeze there had been had died. It was stifling hot in the cabin. I picked my shirt from the floor, used it to wipe the sweat from the hair of my chest and threw it into a corner. Then picked it up and put it on. Not that it made any difference. My fingerprints were all over the cabin. On the tables, the bedstead, on Zo.

I took another drink, thinking about *Señor Peso*. I wondered if Zo had known him. I wished I'd asked her who he was. If Zo had known, she'd have told me. Still, if he hadn't come forward before, I couldn't expect him to step up now. Now only the devil could save me.

What had Zo told me? Not much. She'd told me not to jump to false conclusions. That no one had let me down. That *Señor Peso* couldn't show at my trial without jeopardizing the whole set-up.

It sounded logical when Zo said it. It still did. *Peso* had backed his talk with cash. He'd put up $48,000.00. A thousand a month for every month that I'd spent in a cell. That put him in the big time. International, no doubt. I was only a small cog in his wheel. But I was valuable to him. Why? I knew two dozen fishing boat captains who knew the Gulf and the Caribbean as well as I did. What had he planned for me? Why should he go to the trouble to order a converted sponger to put in and carry Zo and me to Habana?

Not that it mattered now.

24

Restless, my shirt sodden with sweat, I walked into the bedroom again and looked at Zo. She looked cool and somehow at peace. I hoped there were virile men, thick steaks, and aged rum, wherever she was.

Then back of me something metallic 'pinged.' Twisting, I threw myself flat on the floor. Only to hear a bell ring and realize it was the alarm clock. That someone had set for twelve.

I got up and shut it off, thinking about Swede. The old man had been right about a lot of things. If I had listened to him I wouldn't be in this mess. If I'd opened Beth's letter in the warden's office I wouldn't have cared if ten Zo's were waiting.

I'd be in Palmetto City. I'd be in Beth's arms. Or would I? I wished I were smarter than I was. I wished I knew as much about women as I did about fish.

Doubt crept in to torment me. Along with the fear needling my nerves. I closed my eyes and saw Zo drop the letter beside the bed.

"Bah. This woman with whom I used to share you does not love you, Captain Charlie. I am a woman. I know."

I found the letter on the floor and reread it. It was a hell of a letter for a woman to write a man. A man with whom she was supposed to be in love. Setting up covenants and restrictions. If I were sober, if I were ready to settle down, Beth was willing to discuss the matter. Even the 'we'll start all over' had been an afterthought.

I crumpled the letter into a ball and dropped it back on the floor. Then I looked at the clock again. The hour hand had snipped the day from time.

A hundred and some odd miles away, Swede was slipping his hook. At the State's request. Swede was setting out on the big cruise. Swede knew all the answers now.

Not that it would do me any good.

Swede had called this one, too.

"Here, and I mean right here," he'd told me. *"Building up another dividend for the stockholders of Florida Power."*

But why stay to be burned? I hadn't killed Zo. I didn't know who had. I fingered the passbook Zo had given me. I had $48,000.00 in cash. In the National Bank of Habana. That the law didn't know about. If I could get that far, the chances were that I could get farther.

I tightened my belt a notch. The thing for me to do was run. My decision made, I felt better. The law might get me. It might not. But before it did it would have to put on the damnedest man-hunt the Florida west coast had ever seen.

25

As it was, I'd delayed too long. A faint light swept across the screen window. There was only one thing it could be. A pair of headlights bobbing down the sand road leading to the highway.

I blew out the lamp and walked outside. It had been headlights I had seen. Less than a quarter of a mile away. I walked fifty feet from the cabin and stood with my hand in my pocket, in the shadow of a big slash pine. I hoped it was the killer returning.

It wasn't. It was a black and white state police car. With two uniformed troopers in it. The driver slowed as he passed the yellow jeepster and parked in front of the cabin.

His partner got out with his revolver in his hand. "Looks quiet enough to me. Probably a false alarm."

"Probably," the driver agreed. He flicked the car's searchlight around, missing me by inches. "Who lives here?"

"The sergeant didn't have a name. As I get it, it's a rental unit owned by some guy in Cross City."

The driver pointed the searchlight at the shoreline. "Lonely sort of place." He was a bit impatient with his partner. "Well, go ahead. Bang on the door. Wake 'em up and ask 'em if anyone screamed."

His partner banged the screen door. "State Police."

When no one answered, he banged again. Then he opened the screen and walked in, sweeping a path before him with his flashlight. A moment later he whistled. Then light showed in the bedroom window as he lighted the lamp.

"Find something?" the driver called.

"Plenty," the guy inside called back. "That fisherman who called the barracks wasn't whoofing. Some dame was screaming all right. But she isn't screaming now. She's dead."

"How dead?"

"Shot through the head."

"I'll be damned."

"After taking a hell of a beating. And boy is she a little honey."

My whole body drenched with sweat, I waited for the driver to get out of the car so I could sneak away. Instead he talked rapidly into his two-way radio.

"Kaniss and Phillips reporting. On that call to Dead Man's Bay. A dead woman in the cabin where the woman was heard screaming. Shot through the head, Phillips says."

So much was clear. There wasn't another house within a mile of the cabin. No one could have heard Zo scream, if she had screamed. And she'd only screamed three words.

"No. Please, God."

Whoever had killed her had called the police. He really wanted to pin this thing on me. And he hadn't wanted me to get too far away before the law stepped in.

The two-way crackled something and the driver called to the lad in the cabin.

"Any sign of a man?"

"Plenty," the lad inside called back. "Looks like they did plenty. And there's a broken rum bottle on the floor. And a chair tipped over. You know, the usual drunken party." There was a wistful note in the trooper's voice. "I don't know why I never get in on any of these drunken parties. At least not with dames like this one." He repeated, "Boy, is she a little honey."

"Describe her."

"Five feet two, one hundred and ten, well-stacked, black hair, black eyes. Not more than twenty-five. A small mole under her right breast. Probably Cuban."

The driver repeated the description into the two-way, then said, "Check the cottage for her purse, while I call in the plate on the jeep. Funny the guy didn't blow in the car."

"Maybe he's lyin' around drunk somewhere."

"Could be. We'll have a look."

The driver called in the number of the license plate and by that time the trooper in the cottage had found Zo's purse. He called:

"I was right about her being Cuban. Her name is Zo Palmira. According to an Eastern Air Line stub, one way Habana to Palmetto City."

"Anything else?"

"That's all."

The driver repeated the information into the two-way. Then he got out of the car. "Okay. You've seen women before. They're all built just alike. Only some more so than others.

27

Come on out and help me look around until the other boys get here."

The trooper in the cottage opened the screen door lighting a cigarette. "You think he hung around?"

"It's hard to tell what a drunk will do. You think he was drunk?"

"I'd say he was stinking. There's an empty bottle in the bedroom and two more in the kitchen."

They stood a moment in indecision, flicking their lights between the trees. Then I got my first break.

The driver of the car, an older man, said, "I tell you what, Joe. You take a look at the beach. I'll comb the ground around the cottage. You didn't find the gun?"

"No."

"Then watch yourself. And if you spot the bastard let him have it if he even looks like he's going for a gun."

The young trooper followed the path toward the shore. The older man began a wide circle that would bring him directly in front of the tree under which I was standing. Taking the gun from my pocket I stepped back of the tree and pressed my body into the bark.

Then as he passed me I stepped out and rammed the gun into the small of his back. "Don't try to turn and don't yell. And maybe nothing will happen to you."

He played it smart and stood still. "Don't be foolish, chum. I'm the law."

I said, "I know who you are. Drop your hands to your side. I'm going to take your gun."

Sweat starting on his cheeks, he hesitated.

I said, "Or I can plug you first. It doesn't much matter to me."

He dropped his gun. I picked it up and put it in the pocket of my coat.

He said, "Now what?"

I said, "Now walk slowly to the cruiser, raise the hood, and rip the ignition wires loose."

He shook his head. "You can't get away with it, fellow. There are more cops on the way. Three cars full of them."

"I heard you reporting," I told him. "Walk."

He walked slowly toward the cruiser. His back as straight as a Burma rod. Still sweating. But a good copper. "Why did you kill her, fellow?"

"I didn't."

"Then who did?"

I told him, "I don't know. Just some guy who walked in."

28

"You expect me to believe that?"

"No."

"Why not put that gun away and let's talk it over."

"No. Just do what I told you to do."

He lifted the hood of the police car then hesitated again. I reached in and did it for him, ripping loose all the wires I could find.

He said, "All you're doing is building up more trouble for yourself."

I told him the truth. "Brother, I couldn't be in any more trouble than I am. Now walk on over to the jeepster."

"What if I yell for my partner instead?"

"I'll blow your spine in two."

"You say that like you mean it."

"I do."

He walked over to the jeepster. I felt the dash with my left hand to make certain the keys were in the ignition. They were.

"Now what?" he asked.

I considered taking him with me and decided against it. "Now lie down on your face."

There was enough moonlight for me to see the back of his ears turn red. "I'll be goddamned if I will," he said.

He turned, yelling, "Joe!" at the top of his voice, sinking his right fist into my guts as he yelled.

I could have killed him. I didn't. I had nothing against the guy. All he was doing was his job. I brought up the gun instead and laid it alongside of his head. He went down dragging me with him, shouting, "Joe" again.

I fell on top of him, the trooper beating at my head with his fists, blinding me with pain. Forgetting the gun in my hand I swung a hard left to his jaw. Then sunk my knee in his stomach.

He gasped, "Oh, Jeez," and lost all interest in trying to hold on to me.

I wanted to be sick, and hadn't time. I scrambled to my feet and back of the wheel of the jeepster and kicked the motor over. Just as the young trooper pounded up the path from the beach, his gun in his hand but afraid to shoot for fear of hitting his partner.

"Sing out, Ben," he shouted.

Ben managed to get to his knees, vomit dribbling from his mouth. "Shoot the son of a bitch," he wheezed.

A slug starred the windshield of the jeepster. Then another. As sick as the trooper I'd kneed, I swung the jeep in a wide U-

29

turn. The older trooper, on his feet now, showed briefly in the headlights I'd turned on from force of habit.

He screamed as the bumper hit him.

There was a crashing in the brush. Then I turned off the lights and bumped down the rutted road to the highway. At sixty miles an hour. Swaying from side to side. Sideswiping trees. Scrunched down in the seat. The young trooper spraying the back of the car and the windshield with lead.

I made the highway and stopped to be sick. Then started on again. I had at most a five or ten minute start. I'd put the patrol car out of action but the chances were its two-way radio was still working. According to the trooper I'd slugged, three more cars were on their way. I hadn't the least idea which direction they would come from. It would only be a matter of minutes before road blocks would be set up. Before every law enforcement officer in every county on the Florida west coast would be alerted for a killer driving a new yellow jeepster with the license tag 4-1153.

As I remembered, there was a little town five miles down the road on the north bank of a river. I had remembered correctly. The business houses, except for one filling station, were dark.

I'd slowed down for the town. As I passed the filling station a tired-looking elderly tourist driving a mud-splattered '51 Buick with Iowa license plates pulled out and gave me a dirty look as I passed him.

Driving faster now, I drove on to the edge of town and the bridge across the river. There was a small gap perhaps eight feet wide between the black and white guard rail leading up the small ramp and the wooden bridge proper.

Pointing the jeepster at the gap, I rammed down on the gas and hopped out, hitting the road hard, skidding thirty feet, winding up panting with my nose buried in sand. The jeepster crashed through the gap, splintering the guard rail. A moment later it hit the water with a sullen thud, showering water as high as the bridge.

I sat up and held my head as the '51 Buick I'd seen braked on the approach to the bridge and the elderly tourist stuck his head out the partly-opened window.

"Holy smoke, fellow," he gasped. "I thought you were going pretty fast when you passed me. But not that fast. What happened? Did your car go out of control?"

I got to my feet and limped over to the car. "No," I told him. "I did."

30

I yanked open the door and climbed in beside him, ramming the nose of the gun that had killed Zo in his ribs.

"Let's roll. How fast will this crate go?"

He looked at the gun and swallowed hard. "Well, I've had it up to sixty."

I shook my head at him. "Uh uh. Let's open it all the way up. This make and model will do a hundred easy. And I have a date with a road block where this road joins U.S. 19. And there's apt to be some shooting. Unless we get there first."

The old man looked from the gun in his ribs to me. I knew what he was thinking. He didn't want to lose his car. He didn't want to die. If he did as he was told the odds were that he wouldn't.

"I don't seem to have much choice."

"None."

The old man stepped down on the gas. He was frightened but curious. Also a damn good driver. "The law's after you, huh?"

"That's right."

"What did you do?"

It was futile to try to explain. "I killed a woman," I told him.

The old man was philosophical about it as he took a tight S-curve at seventy miles an hour. "Well, of course I don't know the details. But lots of women need killing."

CHAPTER SIX

THERE WAS NO ROAD BLOCK at U.S. 19. We'd beaten the law to the junction.

The old man slowed the Buick and looked down at the gun in his ribs. "Now, what?"

I said, "Turn south on 19."

He grumbled but did as he was told. He was frightened. He was nervous. But behind his fear and nervousness, he was having a hell of a time. For the first time in his life, he was bucking the law. Deep down inside him, he liked it. The buoys and the markers Swede talked about are swell. But most men would

31

rather be on their own. There's a little pirate in every one of us. It's part of being male to *like* to live dangerously.

I added, "But keep it down to sixty from here on. Unless I tell you to step on it."

He asked, "From here on to where?"

I said, "I'll tell you when we get there."

Except for a few night lights in the business houses and filling stations, both Shamrock and Cross City were dark. A lump came into my throat as we passed the grocery store in Cross City. When I'd been in it a few hours before, Zo had been alive, thinking of me. She hated black-eye peas, but she had brought them because I liked them.

Now the peas were burned to a crisp on the stove in the cabin on the shore of Dead Man's Bay and Zo was dead. It still seemed incredible that anyone so vital could die.

"*No. Please, God,*" Zo had screamed, her fragile hands protecting my head. Then, as the red tide had carried us out to sea, her last words had been whispered, "*I love you, Captain Charlie.*"

I wiped my eyes with the back of my hand.

"What's the matter?" the old man asked.

I told him the truth. "I'm bawling."

"You loved her, huh?"

"Yeah. I guess I did."

Eugene, Old Town, Fannin fell under the exhaust. Still without a block. But luck couldn't go on forever. Behind and ahead of me, wires were crackling. Alert state troopers were making plans. Sleepy-eyed small town constables were backing their heaps out of carports. The air waves were filled with me:

'*Red-haired . . . freckles on face . . . six feet . . . two hundred pounds . . . driving a canary yellow jeepster . . . wanted for murder and assaulting a state trooper . . . exercise care in apprehending this man . . . He is armed and will shoot!*'

Troopers were swarming over the cabin by now. Technicians were dusting fingerprints. In a few hours my name and record would be added to the information on the air.

'*Wanted for murder, Charles White . . . released from Raiford yesterday morning after serving a four year term . . . He may be heading for Palmetto City . . . This man is armed and dangerous . . .*'

I fiddled with the radio of the Buick but all I could get was Cuban stations and a glib Texas border announcer who was peddling a vitalized vitamin pill, that, according to him, would cure everything from an inferiority complex to falling manhood.

The old man glanced sideways at me. "You can't get the police band."

"So I see," I told him and switched off the radio.

I rode, looking out the window, watching a south-moon-under skip from the top of one tall slash pine to another. I was still a long way from palm trees. I tried to make some concrete plan and couldn't.

I knew I wanted to get to Habana. I *had* to get to Habana. I had forty-eight thousand dollars waiting for me. More, if and when I reached Habana, *Señor Peso* would probably contact me. If I had been valuable to him before, I was invaluable now. Men who were wanted for murder didn't ask questions about their pay-load. They had nothing to lose.

Chiefland, Otter Creek, Lebanon Station, Lebanon, joined Eugene, Old Town and Fannin as misty blurs in the flat darkness behind the twin tail lights of the Buick. But time was beginning to squeeze me. As we passed through Lebanon the lights in the sub-sheriff's station were on and a yawning fat deputy, buckling on his gun belt, looked up sharply as we passed. The news was beginning to spread. I could expect a block at Inglis. Other eyes had undoubtedly spotted the Buick. All that had saved me so far, was getting rid of the jeepster.

I realized, for the first time, that I was still breathing hard.

The old man rubbed it in. "Time's running out on you, huh?"

I yelled at him. "Shut up. Goddamn it, keep your mouth shut."

He returned his attention to his driving. "You don't need to get sore at me. I just made a statement."

I forced myself to think. I couldn't stay in the Buick much longer. Once we came to a block, it wouldn't make any difference what kind of a car I was in.

If I could reach the Palmetto City waterfront, I knew a half dozen charter boat captains who would be glad to sail me to Habana for a price. The same held true of Sarasota and Fort Myers. Because Beth lived in Palmetto City, the search for me would be concentrated there. My best bet would be to cut into the middle of the state, then west again after I'd passed Tampa Bay.

There was a blue road east out of Inglis. Also a short spur west to Yankeetown and Withlacahoochee Bay. I'd put in there to ice a couple of times when I'd been commercial fishing.

"Not far, now, old man," I panted.

He cocked a gray eyebrow at me.

I lied, "I've got a boat waiting in Withlacahoochee Bay."

33

"Oh," he said. "I see." He tried to keep his voice level. "Which way when I come to the crossroad?"

We were coming into Inglis now. It's a little town, not more than two hundred people, but there is an overhead light at its main intersection and beyond the light I could see the glistening broad side of a black and white state police car.

"We stop right here," I told him. "Pull over on the shoulder of the road and turn off your lights."

He did as he was told. The strain had begun to tell on him. He was panting, too. "Now, what?"

"Now you get out," I said. "You'll find your car unharmed in Yankeetown. That's three miles to your right, at the mouth of the Withlacahoochee River."

He protested, "But—"

I rammed the gun in his side. "Out." There was no use telling him to keep his mouth shut. He'd lie and promise that he would. But he wouldn't.

The old man got out unwillingly, showing his first surface trace of emotion. "You bastard. You dirty, woman-killing bastard. I hope they catch you and burn you."

Like they'd burned Swede at midnight.

The palms of my hands slippery with sweat, I slid under the wheel the old man had vacated and rolled forward without lights, looking for a turn-off. I began to think there wasn't any. I was within two blocks of the black and white patrol car before I found one. It was a narrow dirt lane, flanked by high weeds, leading back toward a clump of live oaks. I parked the car under the oaks and listened. There was no disturbance on the highway. No one had seen me turn off. I took a step away from the car and a cold nose nuzzled my hand. I knew it was a dog. It had to be a dog, but my neck hurt as I craned it to look down. It was a friendly, mildly curious hound. I scratched his ears and walked back to the highway through the croaking of the tree frogs.

As I reached the mouth of the lane, the headlights of a rapidly moving car picked out the frail figure of the Iowa tourist, walking down the middle of the highway toward the road block. The car braked to a screaming stop beside him, and the big deputy I'd seen in Lebanon got out and threw a gun on the old man.

I was too far away to hear them, but from the way the old man was gesturing and pointing, I knew he was telling the deputy about the boat. The officer ordered him into his car. When it had passed me, I followed it toward the block, keeping well in the shadows of the trees and buildings.

34

I hoped the state patrolman would act on the information. He did. He transferred the Iowa tourist to his car and roared off toward Yankeetown. But he was a smart cop. On the chance that I might double back, he left the fat deputy sheriff guarding U.S. 19. Standing beside his parked car under the overhead light, the deputy looked enormous. His shadow was fourteen feet long.

I wriggled across the highway on my belly and skirted the back of a combination grocery and filling station until I was close enough to hear the radio in his car. The lad back of the microphone still didn't know if I had gone north or south and was dispatching his cars accordingly. Then the trooper on his way to Yankeetown radioed in, and the police announcer enthused:

"He's been sighted. At Inglis. On 19. He stopped an Iowa tourist north of Shamrock and forced him to drive him south. Cars 21 and 36 go to Yankeetown and back up Schaefer in 28. He is reputed to have a boat in Withlacahoochee Bay."

I smoked a cigarette in the shadow of a flame vine, listening. Then, moving as quietly as I could, I cut across lots and came out on the blue road headed west. On the road, I turned for a last look at the intersection. From this angle, the deputy wasn't so huge, but three townsmen, armed with rifles had joined him. It was an eerie feeling, being hunted.

For the moment I was safe. Possibly until dawn. With dawn, someone would find the Buick and the hunt would spread out again. There could be only so many boats on Withlacahoochee Bay. By morning, my name and record would be known. I strode on down the state road toward Dunnellon, fifteen miles away. There was always a lot of traffic on U.S. 41. Truck traffic. If I was lucky I might get a ride. If not, I'd steal a car.

I walked on through the moonlight, thinking how a man's sense of values change. Twenty-four hours ago, thinking of stealing a car would have shocked me. Even while I was sitting in a cell doing four years for smuggling. Now it was merely a matter of self-preservation. I was damned if I was going to the chair for a murder I hadn't committed.

It was hot and muggy this far inland. I took off my coat and carried it over my arm. Then I put it on again as protection against the mosquitoes that spewed out of the swamp on both sides of the road.

Sweat trickled into my shoes. The cool, clean freshness of the Gulf was memory along with Zo.

Now and then I passed a farm house. Twice dogs ran out and

35

barked at me. I slogged on through the heat. I couldn't stop. I didn't dare. Then, topping a small rise, I spotted a car with one light and lay down in the ditch that paralleled the road. The car came on with agonizing slowness. It was a battered pick-up truck with two beered-up farm hands in it. They zig-zagged on down the road, happily ignorant that they were about to be pinched for drunken driving; two minor casualties of the murder in the cabin.

The grass was tall and wet and held an illusion of coolness. I lay a long time after the truck had passed, wondering if a man could love two women. Remembering Beth's dainty blonde beauty, trying to feel ashamed for wanting her physically after what had happened, thinking how happy we could have been if Beth had only let herself go the same way Zo had.

But Beth had always been reserved with me. Sex was something that happened after the lights went out, on Tuesdays and Friday nights. I buried my face on my arms and could hear her prim voice in the darkness, "You know I have to work in the morning."

I felt a little sick.

Maybe it was my fault. Maybe a woman couldn't let herself go with a man she didn't respect. Beth had always been slightly ashamed of having married a charter boat captain. Her folks had lived "nice." The material things of life had meant everything to her. A modern house with expensive furnishings, the solid respect of her neighbors, a substantial bank account. A big order for a cracker boy. Until I'd tied in with *Señor Peso*, all I had been able to give her was a forty-year-old frame house on a palmetto and snake-infested island. A three-inch steak at one of the best hotels in town one night and grits the next. She'd even had to take a job with Mr. Cliffton to be able to buy the kind of clothes she insisted on wearing.

It was a wonder she'd written to me at all. Still she had. So she hadn't been overdemonstrative. So what? Why should she be? What more did I want? She'd said we'd start all over. She'd sent me twenty-five dollars to come to her. I'd read her letter roaring drunk with a girl waiting for me. Now the girl was dead and I was running away. I was honest with myself. I was running away, not so much because I was afraid to die, but because I felt put upon, because I wanted one last hell of a good time on the forty-eight thousand dollars I had waiting in Habana.

I began to sweat even harder. What kind of a guy was I?

I wished I could talk to Ken Gilly. Ken was a lieutenant of detectives on the Palmetto City force. He and I had been friends

36

since we'd been yard babies together. In those days his family had lived on the island, too. Ken was smart. He'd gone away to college. He was almost as smart as Swede. Ken could tell me what would be best for Zo, what would be best for Beth. The law wasn't hunting me, personally. The law was tracking down a killer. If I gave myself up and told the story as it happened, they might possibly believe me, find the man who'd killed Zo. I'd promised to love and support Beth. If I turned the forty-eight thousand dollars over to her, she'd never have to worry about money again.

The mosquitoes drove me out of the wet grass. I got to my feet and walked on, starting at unexpected sounds rising above the muted night noises of the swamp.

Then I thought of the bars of my cell. The sweat on my body turned cold. I had trouble getting my breath. I began to walk a little faster, looking back over my shoulder now and then. Right or wrong, I knew what I was going to do. I couldn't stand even one more night back of bars. I'd taken all of prison I could. Right or wrong, I was going to try to reach Habana.

It wouldn't be easy. By morning every patrolman, sheriff, deputy and constable in the state of Florida would be hunting the killer. They would have my name, my habits, my description. If one of them killed me, he'd be a hero. If I killed one of them, I'd be a double killer in the eyes of the law.

There were five hundred and seventy-two hot, hunted miles between me and Key West, and ninety miles of water beyond that to Cuba.

I walked still faster, with my hand on the gun in my pocket, the gun that had killed Zo.

CHAPTER SEVEN

The sign read:

WELCOME TO DUNNELLON
Pop. 1344

I stood leaning on the sign, panting, watching dawn smear the eastern sky a dirty red. Morning was close. I could sense it in the sudden hush. I could smell it in the air.

37

I looked at the darkness behind me. I couldn't take another step. I had to stop. I didn't dare stop. I'd killed a girl named Zo Palmira in a cabin on Dead Man's Bay. At least so the law believed.

My prison-made shoes had rubbed blisters on my feet. I took off my shoes and socks and limped on, barefooted through the silent residential streets, looking for a car I could steal. Most of Dunnellon still slept but, here and there, lights were winking on.

There was a Pontiac parked in front of a white frame house two blocks from the city limits. I tried to jump the ignition, but my fingers shook so badly that I couldn't make a connection. I tried three times. By then, my fingers were slimy with sweat, a family of awakened squirrels were scolding in the tree under which the car was parked, and the street was gray with dawn.

I limped on, breathing hard, carrying my shoes in my hands, looking back over my shoulder, acting guilty as hell, avoiding the business district, trying to find a car with the keys in the ignition. There weren't any. More houses were lighted now. Solid, substantial home men, the type Beth had wanted me to be, yawned their way out onto their lawns wearing pajamas and robes, to pick up the morning paper.

Then the residential street I was on pinched out and I was on a side road again. I started to turn back, walked on. The road led past a dump and came out on U.S. 41, a mile south of town, not far from an all-night truck stop.

There were two cars with out-of-town plates parked in front of it. There were also four big trailer trucks. Three of them had nationally known trucking names and the I.C.C. stamp of approval on their sides. The fourth was a battered gypsy with the name "Jim Kelly-Elyria, Ohio," stenciled on the doors of the tractor.

Just this side of the truck stop there was a small creek under a culvert. I soaked my feet in the water. Then I put on my shoes and socks and looked in both of the cars. The keys weren't in the ignition. I could smell frying ham and eggs and coffee. I hadn't eaten since noon the day before. I fingered the money in my pocket, wondering if I dared stop.

As I looked in the second car, the door of the restaurant opened and an unshaven little man in khaki pants and shirt came out and kicked reflectively at one of the worn tires of the battered truck. His eyes were puffed and red-rimmed from lack of sleep. He looked tired.

The trucker assumed that I'd gotten out of the car into which I was looking and nodded a curt "Good morning."

38

I nodded back as curtly and walked on into the truck stop. Even if I could keep on walking, I couldn't stay on the road any longer. The first police car that passed would spot me.

A big exhaust fan was making a lot of noise inside the combination filling station, restaurant and bar, but it was even hotter than it had been outside. Three truckers and their relief drivers were sitting on stools in front of a white tile counter, eating heartily. A little farther down the counter, two well-dressed couples were toying with their food. They looked like they were sorry they had stopped.

The lad behind the counter was as big as the deputy in Inglis. His sleeves were rolled up above his elbows. His shirt was open at the neck exposing a tattooed eagle hiding in a mat of red hair.

I ordered ham and eggs and grits, and walked on back to the washroom to try and freshen up a bit. The back of my head was still clotted with blood. I washed most of it off, washed my face and slicked down my hair with water. My feet hurt. My head throbbed. But I didn't look too bad. I looked like I'd been on a bat. I limped back and sat down at the counter and the big lad back of it slid a plate of ham and eggs and grits in front of me. It was swimming in grease but it looked and tasted good. It was just what I needed.

The tourists stopped picking at their food, paid their checks and left. The red-haired lad spat after them.

"Goddamn tourists. I wisht they'd stop coming in here." He picked an almost untouched plate of ham and eggs and grits from the counter and pushed it under my nose. "What's the matter with that, mister?"

I said I couldn't see anything wrong with it.

He scowled, "Nor me. Goddamn such picky eaters. What do they think this is, the 'Ronny Plaza'? They make me tired."

One of the truckers winked at me.

The counterman gave him a dirty look and went out to service a car that was honking in front of the gas pumps. I finished the food on my plate and sopped up the eggjuice with my bread. I felt better, but my insides were still quivering. Habana. That was a laugh. After walking all night I was stuck in Dunnellon. The Buick would be found any minute and the search would be extended to all highways.

The counterman finished gassing the car. I ordered another cup of coffee. The trucker in the khaki pants and shirt came in and dropped some silver in the phone. The other three truckers and their helpers finished their breakfasts and left.

The counterman picked six quarters from the tile and jingled them in his palm. "See what I mean? Them kinda guys are real. Two bits every time, even for pie and coffee. And they eat what you put on their plates. Some of them damn tourists ought to take lessons in etiquette from you truckers."

The lad in khaki didn't seem much interested. I'm certain I wasn't. Despite the heat in the truck-stop my undershirt felt cold and clammy. It was all very well to talk about beating your way through a cordon of police. Doing it was another matter.

"Here. Right here," Swede had said. *"Building up another dividend for the stockholders of Florida Power."*

The little khaki clad man ordered another cup of coffee.

"No load, yet, eh, Kelly?" the counterman asked him.

Kelly shook his head. "Naw." He looked at his watch. "I'll give Ocala ten more minutes to make up a load. Then I'm going to dead-head on into Fort Myers. I ought to be able to pick up a load of early cukes or tomatoes and make a market run." He jerked his thumb at the rapidly graying window. "Them big trucking firms is putting us gypsies out of business. I'm working for United Rubber and the finance company."

The red-haired counterman laughed where the cuff of his sleeve would have been if his sleeve had been rolled down. "I should have your money."

I gripped the edge of the counter. If I could get to Fort Myers, I could get to Habana. Both Skip and Harvey berthed in Fort Myers. Either man would sail me to Cuba for five hundred dollars.

"Just come down?" I asked the trucker.

Kelly nodded. "Yeah. From Chicago to Lake City. I was supposed to have a load waiting in Ocala. But I've had trouble with that guy before, so I stuck to 41, figuring something like this would happen."

He ordered and drank another cup of coffee.

I said, "It happens that I'm going to Fort Myers. I'll be glad to pay you whatever you think it's worth to let me ride along."

The little man rubbed his red-rimmed eyes. "Can you drive that rig of mine?"

I was honest. "I've never driven one," I admitted. "But—"

He lost interest. "Sorry."

He finished the dregs of his coffee and dropped more silver in the phone. He was little but he was tough. "All right, nuts to you, then," he concluded his conversation. "I'm not shoving off for New York with half a load for no one. Hell. It wouldn't pay for my ice and gas."

He slammed up the phone, paid his check, laid a half dollar beside his cup and walked out. I followed him into the morning. "I'll give you fifty bucks to take me to Fort Myers."

Kelly opened the door of his tractor. "Why don't you take a bus?"

I said, "Because I'd rather ride with you."

His shrewd eyes took in the prison made suit and crew cut. "Just got out, eh, son?"

He was my last chance. I laid it on the line. "That's right. Yesterday morning."

"And you're hot already?"

"A little." I answered.

"You kidding about being willing to pay fifty bucks to get to Fort Myers?"

I wiped the sweat from my forehead. "No."

"Let's see your money."

I took out my slim roll and counted out five tens.

Kelly weighed them on his palm. Fifty bucks would pay for his gas. It would buy a third of a tire.

"How hot are you, fellow?"

I lied. "Not very. Just a little caper. But I'm out on parole, see? And I don't want to go back."

He put the money in his shirt pocket. "Okay. I'll take a chance on you." He jerked his thumb at the shelf back of the seat. "But you better ride in the sleeper until we get down the road a piece."

I ducked back in the truck-stop and paid my check, then climbed up on the shelf before Kelly could change his mind. As he turned the motor over, he said:

"I don't think much of cops anyway. 'Overweight, overweight, overweight.' That's all they can yak about, especially in Alabama, Florida and Georgia. I get clipped every time I make this run. It's either pay off or be fined."

He rolled the big tractor and trailer out onto the highway, the seven gears forward whining as he shifted, picking up speed. "And for Pete's sake talk to me," he added. "I'd rather have that than your money. I came down without any sleep and I'll probably go back the same way."

I took off my shoes and asked him what he wanted to talk about.

He said, "If it ain't too personal, where did you do your time?"

I told him, "Raiford."

"How long?"

41

"Four years."

"For what?"

"For smuggling."

"I thought that was a Federal rap."

"It is."

"Then how come you do time in a state pen?"

I lay back on the pad. It felt good. "Because of a good war record and it being my first offense, they let me plead guilty to assaulting the Coast Guard officers who boarded me."

Kelly looked at me in the rear vision mirror that supplemented the one on the side of the tractor. "Who boarded you? You're a sailor, then, huh?"

"In a way. I owned my boat. A thirty-eight foot deep sea fishing cruiser with twin screws."

He said, "Well, I'll be damned. What happened to your boat?"

"They confiscated it."

For some reason, it made us friends. "Them sons-of-bitches," he swore. "The dirty sons." Kelly looked in the mirror again. "Like taking my rig away. Tough."

"Yeah. Damn tough," I agreed. "It cost me over ten thousand bucks."

The big job cruising at sixty miles an hour wasn't any worse than riding out a chop in the Gulf, except that the shelf bounced instead of pitched. The rising sun beating down on the metal roof was making me drowsy. I fought to stay awake. I couldn't afford to sleep.

I turned on my left side and elbow and the gun in my coat pocket bored into my hip. I eased my coat out from under me, then froze as a siren began to undulate somewhere on the highway behind us. The police cruiser came on fast and passed us at eighty miles an hour with its siren wide open.

I lay back on the pad, panting.

Kelly wasn't so friendly now. "They wouldn't by any chance be looking for you, would they, pal?"

I had trouble getting my breath. "No. I'm not that important."

"I'm beginning to wonder," he said. "What are you wanted for, chum?"

I asked him if he had a radio in the tractor. He said, "I have. But I never turn it on. The damn thing puts me to sleep."

"Turn it on," I ordered. "See what you can get."

He fiddled with the dial on the dash and tuned in the six o'clock Ocala newscast. The announcer sounded as if he was bug-eyed:

". . . so if you see this man contact the nearest policeman or sheriff's office or call the state patrol. I will repeat his description. He has red hair. He is six feet tall. He weighs two hundred pounds. When last seen, he was wearing a prison made blue serge suit, a white shirt and a green tie. He has no hat. His hat was found in the cabin in which he killed his sweetheart. But he is known to be armed. And this is important. Please pay attention." The announcer stressed the words. "Do not try to apprehend this man yourself. *He has killed once and will, in the opinion of the state police, kill again, before he permits himself to be captured.* Please keep tuned to your local station for further developments in the man hunt. We will interrupt our regular programs to bring you bulletins as we get them. . . ."

Kelly switched off the radio and met my eyes in the rear vision mirror. He no longer looked tired. He was breathing through his mouth, but he was hurt more than frightened, as he looked from my eyes to the gun in the back of his head, then back at my eyes again.

"Cripes," he whispered softly. "And when I ask him how hot he is, he tells me, 'Not very. Just a little caper.' "

CHAPTER EIGHT

IT WAS STILL SHORT of nine o'clock when we raised Tampa. We had passed two road blocks. One at the junction of Florida 48 at Floral City, eighteen miles south of Dunnello. The other just outside Tampa. Both times officers had questioned Kelly.

"Have you seen the man we're looking for? Red hair. Six feet tall. Around two hundred pounds. Probably still wearing a blue serge suit and a white shirt. No hat. Did he try to hitch a ride with you?"

Both times Kelly had pointed to the *No Riders* sign on the windshield of the tractor. Both times he had lied, with my gun at the back of his head. Neither officer had thought to look in the sleeper.

43

The hunt was still unorganized. The law was still confused. The Buick had been found under the clump of oaks at the end of the lane in Inglis, but the law still didn't know if I had left U.S. 19 or whether I'd headed north or south. It did know my name and record and, according to the patrolman who stopped us last, the Palmetto City police had been alerted.

"Not that I think he'll go there," the officer told Kelly. "White would be a fool if he did. The chances are he doubled back and he's somewhere in Georgia by now."

I almost wished I was. Tampa was much too close to Palmetto City. I wouldn't begin to even hope until we'd rounded the bay.

Kelly drove, looking straight ahead, cursing the traffic lights under his breath, damning all dumb drivers, damning me. Twice he almost sideswiped parked cars. The second time I warned him to be careful.

The backs of his ears got red. The muscles of his jaw set. He sat erect in the seat, meeting my eyes in the mirror, coming to a decision. Then, in the first clear space he came to, he pulled over to the curb and cut his motor.

"All right. Goddamn it. You drive."

I said, "Start the motor and get going."

He said, "To hell with you." He opened the door of the cab and got out. In the street, he turned and looked at me. "Why don't you shoot?" He answered his own question before I could speak. "I'll tell you why. Because you only think you're tough. It's taken me a hundred and nineteen miles to make up my mind. Now I know. So lay up there and roast, or try to drive the rig, or get out and walk. I don't care what you do. You've gone as far as you're going with me."

He started across the street toward a bar.

I called after him. "Kelly."

He called back, "To hell with you. I'm going to have a beer. Maybe two beers. On you. I got 'em coming."

He disappeared into the saloon. I climbed down off the shelf and got out of the truck on the far side. Kelly meant what he said. I'd gone as far as I was going with him.

The sun reflecting off the red bricks turned the street into a furnace. The metal door of the cab burned my fingers. I crossed the street and looked in the window of the saloon to see if Kelly was telephoning. He wasn't. The little trucker was sitting at the bar drinking a glass of beer.

The bar looked dark and cool and inviting. I walked on down the hot street wondering if Kelly would notify the police. I

44

doubted it. It would mean more delay for him. Every hour his outfit stood idle cost him money.

At the end of the block, I looked back. Kelly was just coming out of the bar. He crossed the street to the tractor and got in. A few minutes later, he drove by without even looking at me.

It was hot with my coat on. It made me conspicuous. Every other male on the street was in his shirt sleeves. I took off my coat and carried it over my arm. It helped some, but not much. I looked like a guy carrying a blue serge coat over his arm. And the police were looking for a guy, Charles White, wearing a blue serge suit, white shirt, and a green tie. I took off my tie and put ·it in my pocket. The gun in the pocket of my coat was heavy. It banged against my knees. Taking off my tie didn't disguise the fact that I was carrying a blue serge coat.

I stopped in the washroom of the next filling station I came to, and locked the door of the men's room behind me. I wanted to get rid of the coat but keep the gun if I could. I tried stuffing it under my belt between my belly and my shirt. The butt showed between the buttons of my shirt and would show unless I wore the coat. Besides, my belly was wet with sweat and I couldn't tighten my belt enough to keep the gun from slipping down.

Some Joe turned the knob of the washroom door. My heart began to pound. I called "Just a minute." I unbuttoned and dropped my pants and tried to anchor the gun to the inside of my thigh with my tie. It looked like I had a gun tied to my leg. Then the gun slipped out of the tie and clattered on the cement floor.

"What the hell are you doing in there?" the Joe outside asked.

Breathing hard, sweat dripping from my forehead, I put the gun and tie back in the pocket of the coat, rolled up the coat and laid it on the bottom of the oil drum acting as a refuse container. Then I stuffed the soiled paper towels back into the drum. Judging from the general filth of the washroom, it would probably be days before the coat was discovered.

Outside in the street again, I limped on acutely conscious of my red hair. There was a sporting goods store in the next block. I spent a buck and a half for a khaki-colored long-billed fisherman's cap, the kind four out of five tourists buy. I felt like a fool in it, but it hid my hair. It also gave me an idea.

Kelly had stopped close to the heart of town. I walked on, into the main business section and bought a twenty dollar tan gabardine shirt and a pair of twenty-five dollar fawn-colored slacks, in separate stores. I spent five more in still another store

45

for a pair of thick-soled sneakers and a dollar in a drugstore for a pair of dark sun glasses. Counting the dollar I'd spent for breakfast, the four bits I'd left as a tip hoping the fat boy would think of me as a trucker, when the police got around to him, plus the fifty I'd given Kelly, it left me thirty-three dollars and fifty cents of my original stake. But the money didn't matter. If I didn't make Fort Myers, I wouldn't need any money. If I did, either Skip or Harvey would trust me until we got to Habana.

I put the pants and shirt and sneakers on in the washroom of a saloon and stuffed my old pants and shirt and shoes in the bag that the shirt had come in. The new clothes were worth the investment. I still had red hair. I was still six feet tall. I still weighed two hundred pounds. But I looked a lot more like a northern tourist than I did like a cracker fishing guide.

I bought a beer at the bar and sat listening to the conversation. The two men on my right were talking about Joe Di-Maggio. The lad on my left was arguing politics with the bartender. I listened for perhaps ten minutes. The names White or Zo Palmyra weren't even mentioned. It gave me a lot of confidence; more than I'd had. I wasn't important except to myself and the police.

To the general public I was just a small stick in the morning paper. An ex-convict had killed his sweetheart during a drunken brawl. So what? As the old man from Iowa had said, "A lot of women need killing."

Back in the heat of the street, I bought a noon edition of the Tampa evening paper. Then I crossed the street to a drugstore, bought a small canvas duffle bag and put the paper bag in it.

The strain was beginning to tell. I couldn't go on without sleep. I'd make some fool mistake if I did. I was so tired the kettledrums of fatigue were booming in my head. Despite the lift I'd gotten in the bar, I had a feeling everyone was looking at me.

I stopped on a corner and watched the passers-by. The feeling was all in my mind. No one was paying the slightest attention to me. Unless I called attention to myself I was safe for the time being.

At a liquor store near the bus station, I bought a fifth of rum and put it in the canvas bag with my clothes. I wanted a drink and I knew I'd need one to help me to go to sleep. Then I checked into the nearest hotel, using the name of Ben Benson and signing my home address as Chicago.

The desk clerk wasn't even mildly curious. He took my three

46

and a half, racked the registry card and gave a bellboy my key —410.

I followed the boy to the elevator and down the hall to my room. He put the bag on a bench and opened the windows. I gave him a dollar tip and told him to bring up some ice. When he had left the second time, I stripped and showered, wishing I'd bought a razor. I'd forgotten about my beard. It was as red as my hair. I considered having the boy go out and buy me a razor and some blades. Then I thought—to hell with it. I wasn't going to bed with anyone. I'd been.

I opened the bottle of rum and lay down on the bed naked and read the afternoon paper. I'd made a small headline in this one. It read:

EX-CONVICT MURDERS SWEETHEART.

The story was about what I'd expected. I'd been traced back to Raiford through my fingerprints and Beth's letter. I remembered now. I had balled and dropped the letter on the floor of the bedroom.

I read on down the story. Two prison guards and the trusty to whom I'd spoken in the hall, had seen me get into a yellow jeepster with a beautiful black-haired girl. We had, so the newspaper account read, kissed passionately, before we'd driven away. Whoever had done the backtracking had missed the restaurant in Gainesville, but both the liquor store man and the grocer in Cross City had identified me as the man who had been with Zo. The grocer said I was drunk. The liquor man protected his license by saying that we'd both been drinking but neither of us was drunk. He, too, had seen us kiss before we'd driven away.

The trooper I'd tangled with at the cabin had a broken leg, but was otherwise okay. He admitted I'd told him that I hadn't killed Zo, that I didn't know who had, but that angle was played down. The way the state patrol and the Marion County Sheriff figured it, Zo and I had staged a drunken party to celebrate my release. During it, we had quarreled over the letter from Beth. Zo had slugged me with the gaff and I had shot her.

I'd told the Iowa tourist as much. The paper quoted him verbatim:

"I said, 'The law's after you, huh?' He said, 'That's right.' Then I said 'What did you do?' And he said, 'I killed a woman.'"

I was, variously reported, seen on the upper rim of the Gulf near Apalachicola, boarding a Tarpon Springs sponge boat in Withlacahoochee Bay, hopping a southbound freight train at Dunnellon.

I washed my mouth with rum and spit it out. The law was merely confused, not stupid. The man hunt had just begun. Once they sifted out the false reports and the hysterical telephone calls, the net would begin to tighten.

I would be traced to Dunnellon. The lad who lived in the white frame house would report that someone had tried to jump the ignition on his Pontiac. One of the solid substantial men yawning out to pick up his paper from the lawn would remember seeing me. The fat lad at the truck stop would be questioned. He would admit that a man answering my description had been in his place that morning and had left with a gypsy trucker named Kelly who was heading for Fort Myers in the hope of picking up a load of early cukes and tomatoes.

The officers who had stopped Kelly would remember him. Kelly would be located and whether he wanted to or not, he would be forced to talk. He would admit calling my bluff in Tampa. He would name the street and corner where he had stopped his rig. The Tampa police would take up from there.

My coat and tie and the gun that had killed Zo would be found in the refuse barrel. They would learn that I'd bought a long-billed fisherman's cap, a tan gabardine shirt and a pair of expensive slacks. They'd find the bar where I'd changed my clothes. They'd follow me to the bus station. I stopped it there before the cops knocked on the door. Shuddering, I drank from the neck of the bottle, looking at the newspaper picture of Beth's letter, knowing she was reading this, too.

"We'll start all over," she'd written.

I drank from the bottle again. Then I dipped my hand in the pitcher and rubbed cracked ice on my chest, my neck, my head.

"We'll start all over."

I wished I were with Zo. I wished I were dead.

Finally, I slept.

CHAPTER NINE

IT WAS EARLY EVENING when I woke up. A blue bottle fly was droning on the screen. I lay a long time listening to the fly, tast-

into the sweetness of rum in my mouth. It would be dark in a few more minutes. It was time for me to move on.

I had another drink and washed it down with a swig of the lukewarm water in the ice pitcher. Then I called down for a bellboy and sent him out for a razor, some blades, four hamburgers, a quart of coffee and the evening paper.

He grinned at the almost empty bottle on the dresser, when he brought back the things I had ordered. "Kinda pitchin' a little one, eh, Captain?"

"Yeah, kinda," I admitted.

"It does a man good," he said sagely. He added sadly, from the doorway. "That's what I try to tell my wife. But Maybelle don't hold much with drinking."

When he'd gone, I counted my money. I had twenty-three dollars. I walked to the open window and looked out and down. A Greyhound bus marked Tallahassee was loading. As I watched, the street lights came on. Men and women and boys and girls walked into the station. Men and women and boys and girls came out; none of them worried about the law, just going somewhere, coming back, killing time. Still other folks crowded the walk, shopping, walking, talking, laughing, following each other in and out of the stores. They looked like a bunch of ants.

I smeared my bristle with hand soap, put a blade in the razor and shaved. Then I filled the tub with cold water and sat in it while I ate the hamburgers and drank the coffee and read the evening paper.

The state patrol had traced me to Dunnellon. The big lad in the all night truck stop had talked. I read his statement to the reporter who interviewed him after the law had:

"Yeah. Sure I seen him. He was in my place about six o'clock this morning. I thought he was just another trucker, see? But, come to think of it, there were only four trucks around that time. Three of them left before he did. So he must have pulled out with that gypsy trucker named Kelly. But he don't act like no killer to me. He ate every bit of what I served and left me a four bit tip."

I wondered how a killer acted.

Officers Clausen and Dew of the state patrol remembered stopping a thirty-two foot trailer truck driven by a man named Kelly. Both officers admitted I might have been riding on the sleeper shelf, holding a gun at Kelly's head. The Manatee, Sarasota and Charlotte county police were looking for Kelly.

When they found him, I was cooked.

I got out of the tub and toweled. It had been a mistake to stop

49

in Tampa. I should have gone straight on. It was too late to think of that now. The thing to do was to get out of Tampa before the local cops dropped a gill net around the city and netted me along with a lot of hot and bothered small fry. I doubted that the law would figure I'd head for Fort Myers. Once they learned Kelly had dropped me in Tampa, with Palmetto City only forty miles away, they would undoubtedly reason that I would try to see Beth, before I shoved on. Or was that wishful thinking?

My fingers felt thick and blunted. I had trouble buttoning my shirt. The gabardine was hot and scratched my skin. I wished I'd bought a cotton one.

Dressed, I weighted the hamburgers and coffee with the rum left in the bottle and looked at myself in the mirror on the dresser.

I was kidding no one but myself. I looked as much like a northern tourist as a red fish looks like a grouper. I looked like a big, raw-boned, red-haired, freckle-faced fishing guide wearing a silly looking cap, a pair of pleated sissy pants and shirt that was inches too small across the shoulders. No wonder the bell boy had called me "captain". He'd seen me in my hide. He knew me for what I was. I put the dark glasses on. They only made it worse. They made me look like a damn fool.

I threw the glasses in the wastebasket, picked up the canvas duffle bag and rode the cage down to the lobby. There was a new clerk at the desk. He glanced at me, then back at the dog track entries he was reading. I slid the key across the marble and walked on.

The weather hadn't changed. It was still hot. My body perspiration was turning the tan shirt black. I stood a moment in front of the hotel, debating whether to push on for Fort Myers or buy a ticket for West Palm Beach, and then cut back across the state. I decided it didn't make any difference what I did. It hadn't been shrewdness or brains that had gotten me this far. If my luck held, I'd make Fort Myers and, eventually, Habana. If it pooped out, I'd be pinched.

I crossed the street to the bus station. A uniformed policeman was standing in front of one of the entrances. I walked past him into the lunchroom and cut through it to the ticket counter. There didn't seem to be any stake-out in the waiting room. I bought a ticket for Bonita Springs, three stops beyond Fort Myers and asked the lad back of the wicket what time the bus left.

He said, "Seven-thirty."

I had fifteen minutes to wait. There was a magazine rack in the lunchroom. I bought two magazines I didn't want, to kill a little time. Then I walked back and looked at the policeman.

His hands clasped behind him at parade rest, he was rocking heel and toe, admiring the south landfall of a pretty Cuban girl walking north.

She was small but well-stacked with a piquant face and a shining mass of long black hair curling around her shoulders. The way she walked, the bobble of her hips, the proud way she held her head, reminded me of Zo. I watched her up the street, with butterflies hatching in my stomach. I didn't want to hide. All I wanted to do was to sit down some place and bawl.

The Cuban girl merged with the crowd on the walk. I lighted a cigarette and started back into the bus station and stopped. A police car swung into the curb in front of the entrance where the patrolman was standing.

Four plainclothesmen got out. One stood beside the car. One walked directly to the ramp where a bus for Palmetto City was loading. One went into the station. The fourth man, his face vaguely familiar, stopped to talk to the patrolman. He had a deep voice that carried. I heard him say:

". . . six feet, red hair, around two hundred pounds.

The patrolman shook his head. "No. I can't say that I have."

My heart began to pound. I tried to swallow. I couldn't. My mouth and throat were too dry. The police had found Kelly. He'd talked. The police knew I was in Tampa, at least that I had been in Tampa as late as nine o'clock that morning. Then I recognized the plainclothesman. He wasn't a Tampa detective. He was a Palmetto City man, the bailiff of the court in which I had been tried. All he had to do was look up and recognize me.

A group of small boys laughing at some wisecrack one of them made came out of the bus station and started up the street. I walked up the street with them looking back over my shoulder.

The detective who'd entered the station came out faster than he'd gone in. The ticket seller had remembered me.

"*Why, yes,*" he'd told the detective. "*I sold a ticket to Bonita Springs to a guy answering that description, not five minutes ago.*"

The detective said something to the bailiff. He gave the uniformed cop a dirty look, then walked up to the corner where I'd been standing a minute before and looked in the other entrance. The cop standing beside the police car reached over and kicked open the siren. It sounded like all the trumps in the world were wailing because Zo was dead.

51

The small boys stopped laughing. They looked at each other, then at me. They stopped walking and pressed themselves against the wall of the hotel. I was in the middle of the walk, alone. I'd never felt so lonely.

Somewhere up in the business district a siren answered the wail of the police cruiser in front of the bus station.

"You there," the Palmetto City bailiff called. "You. The big guy in the tan shirt and cap. The one carrying the bag. Turn around and let me look at your face."

I dropped the bag and ran.

The bailiff fired a shot into the air. "Stop."

I kept on running. The bailiff shot again. One of the women on the walk began to scream. A man tried to trip me. I hit at him with a clenched fist. The crowded walk behind me was filled with shouts now.

"There he goes. Stop him. Stop him, somebody."

A second, a third, then a fourth shot rang out and rocked the street. One of the detectives was shooting now. He wasn't shooting into the air. A bullet richocheted off the wall beside me and a plate glass window starred, then shattered.

I ran on, panting, sweat making my freshly shaven cheeks burn as if they were on fire.

The cries behind me doubled. I could hear the slap of running feet. "Get the son of a bitch. Stop him, one of you guys."

The hue and cry. They hadn't the least idea who I was or what I'd done. It didn't make any difference. I was running. Get me. A fish had swum out of the school. I was no longer one out of many. I was one. I stood out. Get me. It was normal. It was natural. It was nasty.

More sirens began to wail. I rounded the corner, ripped off the long-billed cap and dropped it in the gutter. Then I angled across the street, cutting in between a steady stream of cars and buses. It was Saturday night. The main drag of Tampa was crowded with shoppers, theater-goers, strollers. I forced myself to walk at a normal pace with the crowd on the far side of the walk.

Then the chase boiled around the corner. I turned with the others to look. A girl standing next to me said:

"Something must have happened."

I tried not to pant. "Yeah. It must have."

The traffic and the crowd on Franklin Street effectively blocked the pursuit as far as the mob was concerned. Then the police cruiser, its siren wailing, nosed around the corner against the light. The bailiff was standing on the front bumper. Both of them had their guns in their hands. Both of them were damning the crowd.

"A stick-up, I'll bet you," the girl said.

"Probably," I agreed.

Some of the crowd stopped to watch. I walked on with the girl, glancing back over my shoulder now and then, idly curious. The Palmetto City bailiff and the Tampa detective were standing on the hood of the cruiser, trying to pick me out of the crowd. Not having any success. Both sides of the walk were jammed with people trying to escape the heat.

The light at the next corner was green. I touched the girl's elbow, helped her across the street. She was young. Not bad looking. Willing to be friendly.

"A guy is nuts," she said, "trying to beat the law."

We were walking past the brightly lighted windows of a drugstore. As she spoke, she looked up at me. The smile faded from her face. She looked at my red hair. Then at my freckles. Then at my sweat-stained shirt and heaving chest. Her upper lip curled away from her teeth. Her eyes went round. She opened her mouth to say something, changed her mind and walked into the drugstore.

To buy a chocolate soda? To phone her boy friend? To open her goddamn pretty little mouth and scream:

"*I saw him. I saw Charlie White. There he goes. There. That big red-haired man without a cap.*"

I had no way of knowing. I suddenly didn't care. My feet hurt. I was tired. My head began to ache again. It was an effort to think, to move one foot in front of the other. I'd run as far as I could. I couldn't run any more. I'd run out of places to run to.

My hand shook as I lighted a cigarette. By this time, the detectives on foot were weaving through the crowd, looking at faces, asking questions. The bus station was plugged. So was Union Station and the airport. Every road out of town was blocked, or would be. With one possible exception—the causeway to Palmetto City. The police would probably leave that open. Like an inverted fish trap. To tempt me to try to go to Beth.

That was all right with me. If I couldn't make Fort Myers and Habana, I wanted to talk to Ken Gilly, tell him I hadn't killed Zo, ask him to keep an open mind regardless of what happened to me. I wanted to talk to Beth. I wanted to tell her how sweet it had been of her to write, how sorry I was that I'd messed up both our lives. Before they took me back to Raiford and put me in the little white house. The one Swede was no longer using.

"*Here. And I mean here,*" he told me.

There was an empty taxi parked in the cab zone a few feet from the corner. I got in and leaned back against the cushion. The driver flipped his flag. "Where to, chum?"

I said, "Palmetto City."

CHAPTER TEN

I'D BEEN RIGHT about the causeway being open. There was no block at either end of it. There was also no way out of Palmetto City except by water or back across the causeways. Three causeways. The man hunt was over. The law had me where it wanted me, now. All it had to do was draw in the net.

Passing the dog track, the cab driver asked, "Whereabouts in Palmetto City, fellow?"

I blew smoke at the ceiling of the cab. I wanted to talk to Ken. But friend or not, Ken would have to arrest me. Ken was the law. And I wanted to talk to Beth before I was locked up.

I said, "Just let me off at the mole."

Palmetto City hadn't changed. The green benches lining both sides of Center Street were crowded with northern tourists. A band was playing in the shell in Phillips Park. Dig Davis, a kid I'd soldiered with, was directing traffic at Fourth Avenue. For some reason he made me think of Matt Heely. Matt owed me a thousand dollars. Matt had a boat capable of raising Cuba. It could be that I could get Matt to sail me to Habana, if I could contact him before I was picked up. I began to hope a little, but not much. After I'd talked to Beth, I might see Matt. It would depend on what Beth advised me to do.

The mole was dark and crowded as usual, with northern tourists fishing for grunts and pig fish about the size of the ones I usually used as bait for snook. I paid off the cab driver with my last ten dollar bill and lighted my last cigarette, while I watched him pull away.

The cops seldom patrolled the mole. I was safe for the time being. I almost wished they had caught me before I'd gotten this far. I wanted to talk to Beth and dreaded to. She would be pleased to get the money. But telling her about Zo would hurt her.

I stalled for a few minutes watching the fishermen. The tide was coming in. The moon was right. You could have caught fish with a bent pin and a doughball. I watched the excited tourists for a moment, glad to have a chance to feel superior about something. Then I cut across Waterfront Park, under the royal palms, toward the return address that had been typed on Beth's letter.

The street was shabby and run-down, on the edge of colored town, not far from Cliffton's store. The address on the letter proved to be a white frame garage apartment on a bougain-villea-tangled alley, behind a square frame rooming house. It was a hell of a place for the wife of a man who'd made the money I had. Shame made me sweat even harder.

There was no police car in front of the rooming house nor, as far as I could tell, any stake-out in the alley. But neither was there any light in the apartment. Then I remembered it was Saturday night. Cliffton's stayed open until midnight. Even working in the office, Beth probably wouldn't be home until after ten o'clock.

I walked back down the silent street toward the mole. Swede had been right about the bloody tide, too. I must have been out of my mind to treat Beth the way I had.

I tried to salve my conscience. Of course, she could be living in the big old house on the island across the deep water channel from the mainland. But she couldn't live there and work in town. At least, not with me in prison. The only way the old house could be reached was by boat. I'd had to run her across every morning when I'd been home. When I'd been away on trips or out fishing the banks she'd always stayed with her folks.

I hoped she'd rented the old place to bring in a little extra income. But the chances were she hadn't. It wasn't flossy enough for tourists. It needed too many repairs. The odds were that nothing but snakes and raccoons and rabbits and field mice had lived on the island for four years.

I watched the fishermen for another hour and walked back. There was a light in the apartment now. As I watched, it winked out. I reconnoitered both the street and the alley more carefully this time. There didn't seem to be a stake-out.

My heart pounding, I walked down the alley. No one stepped

55

out of the shadows to stop me. No one said, "Just a minute, killer."

The stairs leading up to the apartment were on the outside of the building, profusely covered with flame vine. I inched up, step by step, keeping my back to the wall. At the head of the stairs, I reached out and ran my knuckles across the wooden frame of the screen door.

On the other side of the screen, Beth gasped, "Who's there?"

I said, "It's Charlie. Please don't scream. And please don't turn on the light."

Bare feet padded across the floor until only the screen door separated us. After four long years. There was a hole in the flame vine behind me. Moonlight flooded through it, spotlighting Beth's face and slim young figure.

I began to breathe hard again. Not from fear. I'd lied to Zo. This is what I'd dreamed of. But I'd forgotten that Beth was so pretty. Even with her cheeks stained with tears and deep shadows under her eyes, she was beautiful. And at one time she had loved me.

Beth snatched a thin robe from a chair. Then she pressed her nose against the screen. She was almost as breathless as I was. "You shouldn't have come here, Charlie. The police were at the store not half an hour ago. I promised Ken Gilly I'd call him if you tried to contact me."

She slipped the robe over her shoulders but the front of it gaped open.

I said, stupidly, "Then you know?"

Beth brushed a lock of straw-colored hair away from her forehead, her right breast rising with her arm. "How could I help knowing? It was in both the morning and the evening paper." Her mouth began to work. Tears rolled down her cheeks. "Everybody at the store, except Mr. Cliffton, has been 'sorry' for me all day."

I got it off my chest with a rush. "I didn't do it, Beth."

"You didn't do what?"

"I didn't kill Zo."

"It says in the papers you did."

"I don't care what it says in the papers. I didn't kill her. And I didn't open your letter, I didn't realize what it was, until it was too late. I thought you were through with me. I didn't read your letter until after I'd reached the cabin. When I did read it, I told Zo I was through with her, for good. I told her I was coming back to Palmetto City and you. That's when it happened."

Beth stopped crying. "You mean you didn't kill that girl?"

I panted. "No. Someone I didn't see, some man, slugged me with a gaff hook and shot Zo. He meant to kill me, too."

"Who?"

"I don't know who he was. I didn't see his face."

She pressed her nose still more tightly to the screen. Her voice was a breathless whisper. "You expect me to believe that?"

"Have I ever lied to you?"

Beth thought a moment. "No." She shook her blonde curls against the other side of the screen. "No. That's one thing you've never done, Charlie. You've never lied to me." She stepped back and unhooked the door. "Come in," she said softly, "Before the neighbors see you."

Inside the room I tried to take her in my arms.

Beth pushed me away. "No, I want time to think. This may change things for both of us. You swear you didn't kill that girl?"

"I swear it."

From what I could see in the moonlight, it was a one room efficiency apartment with a small kitchenette and bath. Beth sat on the edge of the bed. "Please light me a cigarette, Charlie."

I said I didn't have any. She said there were some on the table. I lighted one and gave it to her. Beth had changed in one respect. It was the first time I'd ever seen her smoke. I sat on the bed beside her. It squeaked slightly under my weight.

"Why did you come here?" she asked me.

I told her the truth. "I didn't intend to at first. I didn't think you'd want anything to do with me. I was going to try to make Habana, but they blocked me off at Tampa."

The bar in the screen door so divided the moonlight that all I could see of her were two small white feet. It was like looking at a surrealist painting. I couldn't see her face but I could feel the scorn in her eyes.

"In other words, if you could evade the law and get out of the country, you were going right back into the same vicious racket that wrecked our marriage. You were going to work for *Señor Peso* again."

I cracked my knuckles. "That's right." I didn't know how much time I'd have with her. I didn't want to waste it trying to explain my involved reasoning. I made it as short as I could. "I made up my mind that if you were waiting for me when I was released, I'd go straight. If not, I'd identify and kill *Señor Peso* for not helping me during my trial."

Beth turned toward me and her warm body brushed my arm. "Then you still don't know who *Señor Peso* is?"

"No."

57

"Then what happened?"

"When I was released, you weren't waiting for me, but Zo was. She told me *Señor Peso* hadn't let me down and proved it by giving me my Habana bank book with a thousand dollars deposited to my account for every month I'd been in prison. She said a boat would put in at Dead Man's Bay and take us to Habana. So I thought 'What the hell' and went with Zo."

Beth protested, "But I would have been there if I could have gotten away. I sent you train fare to come to me." Sobs shook her shoulders. "I wrote you I was waiting. I said we'd start all over."

There was a note of rising hysteria in her voice. I put my arm around her waist. "For Gosh sake, Beth, don't blow your top. Please."

She said, "I'm not going to blow my top." She moved away from me. "But I did write you, Charlie, I did."

I continued to crack my knuckles. "I know. And if I'd read your letter at the prison, none of this would have happened.

"Why did you come to me now, Charlie?"

"To turn the money over to you."

"I don't want it. It's dirty money."

"To say good-bye then. To tell you I was sorry I'd been such a heel."

"Is that the only reason?" Her hand was on my knee.

"To tell you I love you."

"But you loved this other woman, too? This Zo?"

I looked at the small feet in the moonlight. I'd never lied to Beth. I continued to be truthful. "Yes. I did. I loved both of you, I guess."

Beth's fingers tightened on my knee. She began to cry softly. "What will they do to you when they catch you, Charlie?"

I took the cigarette from her fingers and sucked it to a small red torch. "What we're doing to this cigarette."

She sobbed, "I won't let them. If you didn't kill that girl, there must be some way we can prove it."

I snuffed the cigarette. "How?"

Beth shook her head. She was sitting so close that her hair brushed my face. It smelled sweet and clean. The small apartment was hot and filled with the smell of her. I was acutely conscious of her body.

"I don't know," she admitted. "There must be *some* way." She clutched at a straw. "Perhaps Mr. Cliffton could help us."

Cliffton was the merchant for whom she worked. She'd been his confidential secretary for years. Beth liked him. I never had.

A cocky little cracker from the middle of the state, he had built an idea into the biggest business in town. He boasted that he would not be undersold. To my knowledge, he never had been. He was a shrewd merchandiser, a good showman. He wasn't afraid to spend money on advertising. As a result, he'd built a hole in the wall drug store into a block square, four story high merchandise carnival, handling everything from apples to zithers. If you couldn't buy it at Cliffton's, it wasn't for sale.

I asked, "Why should Mr. Cliffton help us?"

Beth took her hand off my knee and folded her hands in her lap. "Mr. Cliffton is in love with me. He's asked me to marry him. He even offered to buy the old house on the island so I'd have money to live on and wouldn't have to work while I made up my mind whether or not to divorce you."

I said, "That's a hell of a note."

Beth said, hotly, "Your own hands are clean?"

The strain was beginning to get me. Too much had happened too fast. I buried my face in my hands. "No. I guess they aren't. I'm sorry. I have no right to say anything. Not after the way I've messed up our lives."

Beth pulled my hands away from my face. I couldn't see her now. She was too close. But I could feel her. "Kiss me, Charlie," she demanded.

I said, "I shouldn't think you'd want me to. After the way I treated you."

Her breath was sweet in my face. "Kiss me," she repeated.

I took her face in my hands and kissed her. Not the way I had kissed Zo. Without passion. Like I had kissed Beth at the altar. After Reverend Paul had finished marrying us. When the world had still been our oyster. Beth was something sweet and beautiful and good. She was something that had been missing from my life for a long time.

When I lifted my head, the shaft of moonlight had risen so I could see her face. Her eyes were shining. Her lips brushed mine, again. "It's going to be all right, Charlie. Believe me. I don't know how we're going to do it. But somehow, we'll *make* it right."

I sat, afraid to move, afraid to touch her. The next move was up to Beth. She sat a long time, just fondling my face with her fingers. Then she leaned back, with her hands cupped under her head. Her eyes were cat-green in the dark.

"Prove that you love me, Charlie."

Prove that I loved her.

I kissed her throat, her lips, her lovely shoulders. Her flesh

59

was hot and quivered under my lips. I touched her and she whimpered.

"It's been so long. I've wanted you so badly."

I rolled over and she kissed me fiercely. Her fingers tangled in my hair.

"Love me. Love me," she panted.

Then a car drove up the alley and stopped. A revolving red police spotlight found the screen door and settled, replacing the moonlight with a bloody glow. Two pairs of heavy feet began to climb the stairs.

CHAPTER ELEVEN

BETH TWISTED away from me and stood panting in the red glow of the spotlight, fighting for breath, as she felt frantically for her robe.

I started to get up.

She stopped me. "Stay there," she whispered.

The climbing feet reached the landing. A man's bulk cut off the red glow. Knuckles drummed on the wood of the screen.

Beth finished wrapping her robe around her. "Yes—?"

"It's Ken again, Beth," Gilly told her. "And Sergeant Strawn."

"Yes—?" Beth repeated. "I've gone to bed."

Gilly sounded tired. "We presumed that, Beth, and we're sorry to disturb you. But we thought you ought to know."

Beth was still having trouble with her breathing. "You thought I ought to know what?"

Bill Strawn said, "Charlie's been spotted in Tampa, Mrs. White. He bought a ticket for Fort Myers, but some of the boys jumped him at the bus station and he ran."

"Oh," Beth said. "I see."

I felt like a fool, crouched on the bed, while Beth fronted for me.

"That was two hours ago," Sergeant Strawn added. "Tampa immediately blocked all roads except the causeways, figuring on funneling him here. And it seems to have worked. They've just picked up a cab driver who says he drove a man answering Charlie's description down to the south mole."

"Oh," Beth said. "I see." She found her mules and slipped her feet in them. Then, reaching behind her, she squeezed my hand and scuffed over to the door. "I'm sorry I can't ask you in, but I'm not dressed."

"That's quite all right, Mrs. White," Strawn said. "We just thought you ought to know."

Ken said, "I wish Charlie hadn't headed back this way. God knows I don't want to make the pinch."

Beth was in control of her breathing again. Her voice sounded cool, almost casual. "Maybe he didn't do it, Ken. Maybe Charlie didn't kill that girl."

Ken said, "Don't be silly, Beth. Of course he killed her. You read the papers, didn't you? They staged a drunken party to celebrate his release. Sometime during it, they quarreled. Maybe over your letter. She hit him with a gaff hook and he shot her."

Strawn said, "That's the way the evidence stacks up. You want us to post a guard in the alley, Mrs. White?"

Beth's shoulders raised as she took a deep breath. "Thank you, Sergeant. I don't think that will be necessary. I doubt if Charlie would be fool enough to come here. Even if he should, I doubt if he'd hurt me."

"No," Ken agreed. "I don't think so, either. I don't think he'll come here. Now that he's gotten this far, he'll probably try to get away by water. And if he should get down to the Glades or the Thousand Islands, we'd never find the guy. What was the name of that guide you once told me owed Charlie money?"

I held my breath.

Beth lifted her hair up and away from her neck. "I don't remember," she said. "I'm too upset to think straight. This has all been a nightmare to me."

Sergeant Strawn was sympathetic. "Of course. You get on back to sleep now if you can, Mrs. White. But you will let us know if Charlie should try to contact you?"

"Of course I will," Beth lied.

Ken fixed it good for me. "Remember, you don't owe Charlie a thing, Beth. He and that Cuban girl did plenty before he shot her."

Heavy feet clumped down the stairs. I was still crouched on my hands and knees. I lay down on the bed, my body bathed in cold sweat. Now everything was wrong again.

Down at the foot of the stairs, a car door opened and slammed. A motor purred. The red light moved away. Beth scuffed into the bathroom and closed the door. After a long time she came out and sat on the edge of the bed. She didn't take off her robe or make any move to lie down beside me. She just sat staring at the screen door.

Swede had been right about so many things. He'd said, *"A man can starve a dame. He can get drunk and beat her every night and twice on Sunday and she'll still think he's her personal Marshall Plan in a silver champagne bucket. But only if she knows that she's the only woman in his life."*

"I'd better go," I said, finally.

Beth seemed to come to some decision. She came down beside me. "No. I don't want you to go. Besides, you're safer here than you would be anywhere else. At least for the time being."

She'd forgotten to take off her scuffs. She inserted the toe of one foot under the sole of the other and the motion brought one of her legs in contact with my body.

"Pardon me," she said.

I said, "That's quite all right."

I was beginning to want her again, knowing she was thinking about Zo. I laid my hand on her arm. "I love you, Beth."

She put her hand in mine. "I love you, Charlie. But you've made it so difficult."

I said, "I know. Maybe I'd better go. I don't want to involve you."

Beth sighed. "No. Why shouldn't I be involved? You're my husband." Her free hand fondled my face. Then her body began to shake as if she were crying or giggling. I decided she was giggling.

"What's so funny?" I asked her.

She said, "You know what I was thinking about when we were so rudely interrupted?"

"What?"

"That you better stay right here in the apartment until after I talk to Mr. Cliffton. No one ever comes here but me. But now that's out. When you don't show up at the police blocks and none of your old friends on the waterfront see you, someone is bound to get nasty-minded and suggest that Ken search my apartment."

I kissed the tip of her nose. "Then the best thing I can do is give up."

Beth shook her hair in my face. "No," she said. She seemed to have a lot of faith in the guy. "Not until after I've talked to Mr. Cliffton. But there's only one logical place for you to hide."

I asked her where that was.

Beth said, "Out at the old house. You know it and the island better than anyone else. An army couldn't find you there, if you didn't want them to." She moved closer to me. "Now tell me just what happened in that cabin, Charlie. And don't try to spare my feelings. My knowing exactly what went on can be very important to us both." She rolled away from me and to her feet. "But first, let's have a cigarette."

She lighted one for both of us, then came back beside me.

Wanting her became a pain. I tried to take my hands away from her. I couldn't. Beth was holding them against her. I blew smoke at the ceiling.

"There isn't too much to tell. We hit the cabin just before dark. Both of us were pretty drunk. We'd stopped in Cross City for groceries and more rum. The Gulf looked good to me. I thought I'd have a swim while Zo got supper, and I did. But I stayed in the water longer than I'd figured and it was dark when I got back to the cabin. Zo had lighted two lamps. One in the kitchen. The other in the bedroom. The coffee water was boiling along with the pot of peas. I'd stripped in the kitchen before I'd gone in the Gulf. My clothes were still lying on the floor. I was still so drunk that I tripped over them. Then I saw your letter and remembered that since the riot all incoming mail had been retyped."

Beth's hand tightened on mine. "That's why you didn't read it at the prison?"

"That's right. When I did read it, I was sick. I walked on into the next room and told Zo we were through, that I was coming back to Palmetto City."

"What was she doing?"

"Nothing. She was in bed."

"What did she say when you told her you were through?"

"She thought I was joking."

"Then what happened?"

"She wanted to read your letter."

"You let her read my letter?"

"Yes. I did."

I could feel Beth's body stiffen. "What did she say when she'd read it?" she asked.

"She said you didn't love me."

Beth kneaded her arm with my fingers. "If I didn't love you, do you think you'd be here now?"

"No," I admitted. "I don't. I knew you loved me then, I think. But I was still half drunk, confused. And Zo pointed out that all I knew was the water, that I couldn't make a dime on land."

I began to sweat again. "Well—"

There was enough moonlight to see Beth's eyes. They were cat-green and slitted. "She persuaded you to make love to her."

"Yeah. Yeah. That's what happened."

"Then where did the quarrel come in?"

"There was no quarrel. All of a sudden the corners of Zo's mouth turned down. She screamed, 'No. Please, God.' She clasped her hands on the back of my head and the next instant the whole ceiling fell on me. I turned, but all I could see was a white blur. Then the guy hit me again. As I passed out, I remember hearing a shot. When I came to, Zo was dead."

"But it was a man who hit you?"

"Yeah. It was a man. I'm positive of that."

The name was distasteful to Beth. "This Zo person had mentioned some other man?"

"No. She said there'd been no other man since I'd gone to prison."

Beth's lips twisted in the moonlight. "I can imagine."

I didn't say anything.

Her free hand caressed my face again. "You've told me the truth now, Charlie?"

"Exactly as it happened."

"You didn't kill her?"

"No."

Beth was suddenly crisp and businesslike again. She might have been fully dressed and sitting behind her typewriter in Mr. Cliffton's office. "All right. I'll tell Mr. Cliffton everything you've told me in the morning."

I still didn't like the Cliffton angle. I said so. "You say the guy loves you. You say he's asked you to divorce me and marry him. What's his reaction going to be when you tell him you've talked to me. Cliffton's going to reach for his phone and call Ken. The guy is a bargain hunter. And it's a lot cheaper for him to turn me in to be burned than it is for him to pay for a divorce."

Beth put her fingers on my lips. "You're doing Joe, Mr. Cliffton, a big injustice, Charlie. He's really a very fine man. An honorable man."

"I'll bet."

"I mean it. You might as well accuse Mr. Cliffton of being *Señor Peso* as of being capable of doing such a thing as you just said. Besides, I'm not going to tell him where you're hiding. You have to admit he *is* smart."

"Yeah. He's that, all right."

"All I'm going to tell him is that I don't think you killed the

64

girl and ask his advice on how to go about hiring a private detective to prove it. This Zo was a Cuban, wasn't she?"

"Yes."

"Pretty?"

"Very."

"Then maybe it was some lover who followed her from Habana. I mean who killed her and left you framed for her murder. The police won't believe us. Not even Ken. I·realize that. But if a private agency man could uncover some jealous lover, we'd at least have something tangible on which to base our contention."

I kissed her eyes. "Thanks for believing me, Beth."

"You're my husband. It's my duty to stand by you."

My fingers crawled down her back. "That your only reason?"

She began to have trouble with her breathing. "No. I love you. You should know that by now, Charlie. And you'll hide out on the island until after I've talked to Mr. Cliffton?"

"I will. But how will you contact me?"

She gasped as I touched her. "I'll find some way. I have a right to go out there anytime I want to. Maybe I want to put the house in order, to be sold." She turned on her side and nibbled at my lower lip.

I continued to caress her. "When do you think I'd better go out?"

Beth panted. "About four o'clock this morning. There won't be any moon then. The searchers will be tired."

"And until then?"

"Do I have to say?"

She didn't.

CHAPTER TWELVE

I DRESSED in the hot sticky silence. I couldn't find one of my shoes. Beth found it under the bed. She handed it to me. I put it on and lighted a cigarette.

65

I'd wanted to see Beth. I had seen her. Even with every cop in Florida looking for me, I should feel a glow. I didn't.

Beth had changed.

There'd been some other man in her life while I'd been gone. She wasn't the same girl I'd left. Beth knew all the answers now.

"Why so silent?" she whispered.

"Just thinking," I whispered back.

She kissed the lobe of my ear.

I fought the queasy feeling in my stomach. I had no right to be jealous. I'd forfeited all rights. And Beth had given them back again.

I forced myself to put on my shirt. I wanted to stay. I felt as though Beth wanted me to. But Ken Gilly was nobody's fool. When I wasn't picked up by morning they'd know I was holed up somewhere. Beth was my wife. Her apartment was the first place they'd look.

I walked to the screen door. Beth padded barefoot beside me. "Have you a gun, Charlie?"

"No."

"Wait."

She padded back through the dark. I heard a dresser drawer open. Beth pressed a gun into my hand. From the feel, it was a .32 Colt automatic. I put it in my side pants pocket.

"Don't use it unless you have to."

"No."

"How about cigarettes?"

"I took two packs from the table."

"Good." Beth stood on her tiptoes and kissed me. "I'll be out tonight or tomorrow night at the latest."

"What if you're followed?"

"I won't be. I'll make certain I'm not."

"Ken is going to be suspicious."

My shirt was open at the neck. Beth twisted a tuft of the hair on my chest until it formed a tiny peak. "Pooh for Ken Gilly. I can twist Ken around my fingers."

I wondered if Ken was the man in her life. I took her bare shoulders in my hands and kissed her. "Be careful."

Beth kissed me without passion, pressing the length of her body against mine. "You be careful. Please."

My fingers bit into her shoulders. "Say it."

Her lips brushed mine again. "I love you, Charlie."

"I love you, Beth," I told her. Then I unhooked the screen and keeping my back to the wall I sidestepped slowly down the stairs.

The moon had set. It was even hotter than it had been. It was like moving through warm black ink. The only sound was the drip of condensation and the occasional rustle of a dry palm frond.

At the foot of the stairs, I stood with my back pressed to the wall, wondering if it was worth it to try to make the island. My body felt like an empty rain barrel. I was emotionally and physically drained. Instead of feeling free and eager to run on, somehow I felt trapped.

I moved cautiously up the alley, feeling my way toward the distant street light I could see. A hundred feet from the foot of the stairs I stopped, poised on the balls of my feet, as a man stepped out from behind the squat bole of a pineapple palm and flashed an electric torch in my face.

His voice was a husky whisper. "Just a minute. What's your name? What are you prowling this alley for at four o'clock in the morning?"

My stomach turned over slowly. Sergeant Strawn and Ken had been humoring Beth. Despite the fact that she'd refused one, they had posted a guard. It was the logical thing to do. I looked at the man back of the flashlight. I couldn't see his face. All I could tell was that he was big. But he was obviously new to the force, at least since I'd been away. Otherwise he would know me. My only chance was bluff and run.

"Why, my name is Fred Davis," I told him. "And I'm not prowling the alley. I live five houses back. I'm on my way down to the bay to fish the morning tide. Why? What's the big idea of popping out from behind a tree and scaring a guy to death?"

"Wise guy," he whispered. "Wise guy."

I caught a glint of silver back of the light. I thought at first he was drawing a gun. Then his arm swung down and back. I knew then what he had in his hand. I backed a step and allowed the weapon to rip air. Then before he could set himself again, I stepped in fast and swung a hard right to his jaw. The flashlight flew from his hand and winked out. He stood a moment, a darker blob against the night. Then, as his knees collapsed, he grew smaller and smaller until he melted into the dark of the alley.

I struck a match and leaned over him. His face didn't tell me a thing. He was a stranger to me. But, whoever he was, he was not a plainclothesman. A plainclothesman would have no reason to whisper. Besides, if he was a cop, he was the first one I'd ever seen armed with a six-inch fish knife.

I struck another match, intending to go through his pockets

67

for some clue to his identity, but blew it out as a light came on in a window of the garage apartment under which I was standing. The voice was feminine, thin with sleep and crotchety with age.

"Who struck that match? Who's down there in the alley?"

I purred, "Me-arrh."

"Oh," the old lady said. "Bad kitty."

The light in the window went out. I tiptoed up the alley before the old lady, composing herself for sleep, realized that cats don't strike matches. When I reached the corner, I looked back. As I turned, the light in the window came on again, and the old lady looked out and down. She began to scream.

A low-lying fog hugged the water. The tide was still full, but beginning to ebb. I lay a long time in the sea oats along the shore studying the situation. Here, back of the string of bait camps and boat slips, I was on familiar ground. I knew every pile, every piece of planking, extending out over the tide flats.

Cook's and Robert's were dark. But there was a light in McNeely's bait shanty. As I watched, a young cop, his blue shirt wet with sweat, his cap pushed back on his head, walked out on the pier slapping at mosquitoes and peering into the dark and fog. I moved up the shore toward Frenchman's Bayou and Bill's boat basin, where most of the fishing guides berthed their boats. Four of the cabin cruisers were lighted as late poker games continued or charter boat captains checked over their gear and tackle.

I felt even more trapped than I had at the foot of Beth's stairs. I was back in a cell again. This one of my own making. There were a half dozen boats in the basin capable of reaching Habana. Their captains would sail me there if I offered them sufficient inducement for them to thumb their noses at the Coast Guard. But I'd promised Beth that I'd wait on the island until she talked to Mr. Cliffton.

The more I thought of it the screwier it sounded. Why should Mr. Cliffton do anything for Charlie White? He didn't want to go to bed with me. He wanted to go to bed with my wife. Or had he already been?

I rounded the bayou to Frazer's camp. A dozen rental row boats bobbed at their ropes, as the outgoing tide sucked and gurgled around the piling. I considered stealing a boat, but I didn't. For two reasons. One; a boat would be missed. The only way I could hide it after I reached the island would be to stave in the bottom and sink it. I knew how most bait men felt about their boats. Frazer was no exception. He would raise hell if a

68

boat turned up missing. He'd rather lose his wife than a boat. A good boat cost a hundred dollars. He could get married for five.

Two; a boat crossing the channel might be spotted.

I stripped off my clothes and piled them on a dry plank. Then picking up the plank, I waded out in the water until it was up to my chest. The water was as warm as the air. I swam out into the bay pushing the plank ahead of me.

It felt good to be back in the water. I swam for a long time, then turned on my back and floated, one hand on the plank.

The knife man worried me. Who was he? How had he known that I would be coming down the alley? Why had he tried to kill me? At whose orders? I wondered if he'd been the man who had killed Zo.

My heart began to pound. I should have kicked the son of a bitch in the teeth, made him confess. On the other hand, if he'd been the man in the cabin, he'd have known me on sight. He'd have ripped out my guts with his knife without bothering to ask questions.

I turned over on my face and swam. The morning sky was gray when I sighted the mangrove trees fringing the island. I felt for the bottom. There wasn't any. The storms of the last four years hadn't changed the coastline. Deep water extended to within a few feet of the shore. I pushed the plank up on the beach, then squeegeed and slapped my body dry before I dressed. Sometime during the crossing, my sneakers had fallen off the plank.

Dressed, I sat under a cabbage palm and smoked a cigarette before going up to the house. Now I was really home. My rotting nets, unused since before I'd gone into the army, still hung on their long cypress drying racks, not worth stealing. A half dozen hulks and stove-in row boats lay half-buried in the sand, including the bare ribs of the fifty-footer that had been my father's boat. I was glad the old man was dead.

I looked back toward the mainland. There were no running lights in the channel. As far as I could tell, my passage had been unobserved. When I wasn't picked up by morning, Ken and Sergeant Strawn would undoubtedly make a perfunctory search of the island. But I knew it from one end to the other, all five hundred tangled acres of it. I could hide out for a month, if need be. I could live on rabbits and fish.

I no longer felt tired or depressed. I was home. I'd been with my wife. I had plenty of smokes. Nuts to the law. Let them try to find me.

I got to my feet and padded up the weed-grown path to the house. The path was a jungle of tangled vines. I wriggled through them being careful not to disturb them any more than I had to. I hoped I wouldn't step on a snake.

The old mansion was still picturesque although even in the half-light of dawn, I could see the twenty-foot wide front porch was sagging badly in spots, its pillars rotted away. Its only support was the thick-trunked purple bougainvillea vine that had been old when I was born.

I picked an orange from a gnarled tree, cut a hole in it with my pocket knife and tried to suck it. The grove was as sour as the soil. I spat out the juice and looked at the house again. Beth had never liked it. She'd hated living on the island. She said it was 'cracker.'

I walked up the sagging stairs and onto the wide front porch, watching a flock of white heron wading in the shallows, trying not to think of Zo.

Zo would have clapped her hands and said, *"How lovely."* Zo would have loved the old house as I loved it. So it was 'cracker'. My people had never asked a thing of anyone except to be left alone. The old house represented a people and a way of life that would never exist again. A free, self-sufficient life before society, in an attempt to weaken the strong and strengthen the weak, had set up the goddamn buoys and markers that Swede had talked about.

In the death house it had sounded good. Swede had thought he meant it. But if the clock could have been turned back, and Swede could have started all over again, the chances are he'd have led the same life that he had. Some guys just didn't fit into the new pattern. Some guys were born to take chances.

I sat on the rotting canvas of a chaise lounge and watched the mainland grow out of the channel. I didn't want any part of Mr. Cliffton. I'd been a fool to agree to let Beth talk to him. No private detective could prove that I hadn't killed Zo.

When Beth contacted me, I'd tell her to arrange passage for me with Matt Heely or one of the other guides. To my original destination, Habana. Beth could join me later. I could change my name and buy a house and a boat in Habana. Or Santiago de Cuba or one of the smaller towns. Fish out there. I didn't have to contact *Señor Peso*. We could live well and legally for years on my forty-eight thousand dollars. If Beth loved me, she'd agree. I breathed hard, just thinking of her. And Beth did love me. She'd proved that.

Thinking of Beth made me restless. I tried the big front door.

It was closed but not locked. I opened it and walked in. Closing the door behind me, I took two steps into the dusty silence and stopped.

I think even then I knew. But all I thought at the time was—
I'm not alone in this house.

CHAPTER THIRTEEN

I SLIPPED THE GUN Beth had given me from my pocket. It was on safety. The clip was full, but there was no shell in the chamber. I pumped a shell into the chamber and padded barefoot through the big living room down the long hall to the kitchen. The kitchen was festooned with cobwebs and as dusty as the front of the house. The sun was high enough now for me to see there were no tracks in the dust except the ones I was making.

I looked through the back door. Flame-vine practically covered the glass. The island vegetation had encroached on the rear of the house until the backyard was a jungle of wild grape, live oak, flowering yucca, and re-leafed poison ivy. I tried to open the door and found it was stuck fast by the flame-vine that had grown around the knob and anchored it.

I walked across the kitchen to the rear stairs and plowed a pine sliver with my big toe. I stuffed the gun in the waist band of my slacks and sat down on the floor to dig at the sliver with my knife. I'd have to find shoes of some kind. They'd made me wear shoes at Raiford. All the time. The quarter-inch callouses on my feet were gone.

I extracted the sliver and limped up the back stairs. There was no one in the bedroom that Beth and I had used. Dust lay thick and undisturbed on the floor. The bed was as Beth had left it, stripped to the bare mattress. It was the same with the other three bedrooms. Nothing had been touched. Nothing had been stolen. That was because I was Charlie White. If I'd been a northern tourist who had built a new home on the island and then gone away for four years, the boys would have 'borrowed' everything down to and including the plumbing and the foundation blocks.

I sat on the bed in the front room. The feeling that I wasn't

71

alone persisted. But not as strongly. I put the gun back in my pocket and lighted a cigarette. Nerves did funny things to a man. I finished the cigarette and snuffed it. It was time for me to think of a place to hide. When I wasn't picked up in town or found at Beth's apartment, Gilly and Strawn would either hook up a kicker or get the Coast Guard to run them over to the island. I'd want a vantage point from which to see them coming.

I thought of the captain's walk and dismissed it. It was exposed to the weather. I doubted that the rotted floor boards would hold me. Besides, if I were seen on the walk I'd be trapped. The best place to hide would be out on the island itself. But I'd have to have shoes of some kind.

Then I thought of the old pair of sneakers I'd discarded on my last trip down to Shrimp Bay. I'd left them in the bedroom. I'd told Beth to throw them out. They were probably up in the attic along with the other junk she saved. The attic was the only feature of the house Beth liked. She never threw anything away on the theory that sometime she might find a use for it. This was one of the times.

I got off the bed and looked through the shutter to the mainland. I could see it plainly now. There were three boats in the channel, all of them headed out into the open gulf, probably with charter parties. I wondered what was running. It was too late for king or tarpon. But the gulf was filled with fish. They could be out for almost anything.

As I climbed the stairs, I wondered if there were a hell and if there were what it was like. *"I'll save you a brunette,"* Swede had offered. He didn't need to bother now. I had Zo waiting.

Man. A funny proposition. I'd just spent hours with my wife. Beth had done everything a woman could to prove that she loved me. And here I was thinking of Zo again, almost as much as I was of Beth. Maybe I was a born heel.

The house had been built by my grandfather's father when the law had finally driven the wreckers out of Key West. Both labor and lumber were cheap. Rumpus rooms hadn't been heard of in his day, but the old man had finished the attic as a ballroom so he and his friends could dance when a fleet of small boats had sailed out from the mainland or a rare passenger boat on its way to Cedar Keys, which had been a world port in those days, had dropped anchor in the deep channel to broach a few casks of rum and pay its respects to old Captain White, the last unreconstructed rebel.

The finished section of the attic was thirty by forty feet with two large dormer windows on each side and two smaller windows on each end. But the windows had been boarded up for years. Even when my father had been a small boy, the attic had become a family catch-all and a place to play on rainy days.

It would be dark in the attic. There was a lamp on the dresser. I shook it. It still had some oil in it. I wiped the dust from the bowl and chimney and touched a match to the wick.

Holding the lamp ahead of me, I climbed the narrow stairs to the attic and pushed open the heavy door. A sudden gust of wind slammed the door shut behind me. I took a step into the attic and stopped.

I had been right. I wasn't alone in the house. There was no wind in the attic. A human hand had closed the door. I smelled them, then, the sour stench of unwashed bodies. The smell of men who had lived with fear for a long time.

I was holding the lamp in my right hand. I set it on the floor and reached for the gun in my pocket. From behind me, muscular hands closed around my wrist and shoved my hand deeper into my pocket, making it impossible to draw the gun.

I looked out beyond the faint glow of the lamp. Sitting on folding cots against the wall, a dozen men looked back somberly. I'd seen their faces before. Many times. Always covered with a fine sheen of sweat. On the quays and in the bars of Habana, Port au Prince, Tiburon, Roseau. The faces of men without countries and passports. Hunted, worried, harried men. Men who begged you to name your own price to sail them to the States.

Wetbacks on the grand scale. The most profitable item in the trade. The one thing I'd refused to run for *Señor Peso*.

I tugged at my wrist. "What the hell?"

A thin-faced man with a heavy accent said, "Make out that light."

They were the only words spoken. A man scampered across the floor like a rat, scooped up the lamp and blew down the chimney.

I beat at the man holding my wrist with my free hand. He whimpered with pain, but held on. There was a scurrying sound in the darkness. A wave of men swept over me. Hitting, clawing, kicking. I got the gun out of my pocket and managed to fire one shot. Then the gun thudded to the floor, as a dozen fists pounded at me. I went to my knees, fought back to my feet, then doubled up screaming in agony, as a pointed shoe caught me between the legs. I sensed the circle of men move back to let me fall. Then another foot found my jaw.

I came to, lying in semi-darkness. My nose was pressed into dank earth. There was a rope around one of my wrists and a foul tasting gag in my mouth. I rolled over on my back and spat out the gag. Heavy feet walked over my head. I turned my head to one side. Twenty feet away a trickle of bright sunshine was forcing itself through a thick tangle of vegetation. I'd been in the attic when I'd been slugged. Now I was lying under the house.

I slipped the rope from my wrist and lay listening to Sergeant Strawn's voice, muffled by the double flooring.

"Charlie's been here, all right. We should have come out last night. The dust is thick with his tracks. Barefooted, too. He must have swum over from the mainland."

"He must have," Ken Gilley agreed.

The feet tramped through the house. I started to crawl out, thought better of it, and lay waiting for the shouts and burst of shots when they discovered the men in the attic. I waited a long time. There were no shots. There were no shouts. There could be only one explanation. The men in the attic were gone.

I looked at the length of rope. Then feet tramped over my head again and out onto the sagging front porch. The voices were plainer now.

"Damnedest thing I ever saw," Ken said. He sounded puzzled and a little worried. "I don't get it. I don't get it at all."

From down on the shore, someone called, "White been here?"

"It looks like it," Ken called back. "But that's only half of it. There are a dozen cots up in the attic."

"Cots?"

The lad on the shore said he would be damned.

Strawn said, "It looks to me like some of the boys have been using the house as a drop for wetbacks."

There was the scratch of a kitchen match as one of the two men lighted a cigarette. Then Ken admitted, "Could be. Some of these damn fishing guides will do anything for money. Either way, Beth's going to have a fit when she hears this."

"Yeah. Probably." Strawn said. "But you never can tell about a woman. You think Mrs. White was leveling with us last night?"

"How do you mean?"

"I mean it's funny we didn't pick White up last night. It's only a few blocks from where the Tampa cab man dropped him over to her apartment. Maybe he was in the apartment while we were talking to her. It wouldn't have taken a minute to slip into something and invite us in. But she didn't. She didn't even turn on the light. Then this morning there was that fracas in the alley not a hundred feet from her stairs. So there was no one there when the prowl car answered the call. It could have been White and one of his pals that old Mrs. Pilley heard."

"I don't know what to think," Ken said. "Beth's sworn right along that she'd never have anything more to do with Charlie on account of that Cuban girl. Then she writes him a letter saying she's willing to start all over. Like you say, you never can tell about a woman."

The lad down on the beach called, "So what do we do now?"

"I'll be damned if I know," Ken admitted. "If I know Charlie, and I do, he's long gone by now. But while we're here, we'll look around."

He walked down the sagging stairs and kicked at the tangled vegetation growing up around the house. I pressed my belly to the sand. A moment later, he squatted and looked under the house. I could see Gilly but he couldn't see me. Ken hadn't changed. He was still round-faced and over-plump. He still wore rimless glasses. He still looked more like a bank teller or a preacher than he did like a lieutenant of detectives.

Sergeant Strawn was a little smug. "We should have come out last night. Remember, I said Charlie would probably head for the old house."

Ken had always had a temper, even when we were boys. He still had one. Releasing the vegetation his hands were parting, he stood up. "All right. You told me. You thought he might head out here. I didn't. I didn't think he'd be that big a fool. So you were right and I was wrong. *If* those footprints do belong to Charlie. Can you prove they do?"

Sergeant Strawn attempted to placate him. "No. I can't, lieutenant. And last night was just a lucky guess on my part. *If* it was Charlie who made those footprints in the dust."

A moment of silence followed. Then Ken said, "Well, I suppose we'd better go back and get some of the boys and search the island. But personally, I think it's a waste of time."

"How come?" the voice from the shore called.

Ken told him. "Charlie would be a fool to stick around so close where everybody knows him. If there is any truth in that *Señor Peso* gag he sprang at his trial, some of *Peso's* boys were probably waiting for him here. That would explain the cots. Charlie buying a ticket for Fort Myers could have been a red herring. He could have been headed here all the time. There are three coves on the other side of the island where I know a good sized boat could anchor. And the chances are, when he got here, he took off with the party waiting for him."

75

Sergeant Strawn continued to butter his stripes. "Could be. Sounds logical, lieutenant."

Ken allowed himself to be placated. "Well, let's get back to the mainland and ask the chief what he thinks we ought to do. If there's any chance that the island has been used as a port of illegal entry, he may want to call in the Federal men."

Their voices trailed off as they walked down the path to the shore. A few minutes later a kicker roared as it caught, then settled down to a high-pitched drone as they pointed the boat toward the mainland.

I crawled to the edge of the house and looked out. They were using one of McNeely's boats. Strawn and Gilly were sitting on the middle thwart with a youthful uniformed policeman handling the outboard motor.

I lay watching the boat grow small. The attack on me in the attic was easily explained. So it was my house. I wasn't supposed to be here. I was supposed to be in police custody by this time, accused of murdering Zo Palmyra. I'd poked my nose in where it didn't belong. Being alive was another matter. The only way I could explain that was that the men who had attacked me had been about to tie and weight me and drop me into the channel, when they had been interrupted by the arrival of Strawn and Gilly. In panic, they had rolled me under the house and scattered into the brush.

I picked up a rock and waited. I waited for half an hour. Then I crawled out and went inside the house. It was as silent as it had been the first time, but the feeling I'd had before was gone. I tiptoed up the stairs to the attic.

The door was open. There was no one in the attic. Except for a dozen canvas cots there was no sign that anyone ever had been there.

I climbed the ladder to the top and muscled myself up onto the captain's walk. From where I stood, I could see every section of the island. There was no wind. The palm fronds drooped in the sun. There was no sign of movement or motion. As far as I could tell, there was no one on the island but me. But on the far side, nosing its way out of one of the coves Ken had mentioned, was a white thirty-eight foot double cabin cruiser with a flying bridge. The boat was new to me. I wished I had a glass so I could read its name and registration number. Out in the gulf proper, it headed north toward Tarpon Springs. I wondered if my friends in the attic were on it. I hoped so.

76

CHAPTER FOURTEEN

THE MORNING SUN got hotter. I stood letting it bake my sore muscles, looking alternately at the gulf and across the channel to Palmetto City. I should have been depressed. I wasn't. For some reason I felt fine. I wanted to contact Beth; tell her to stay off the island. But I was stuck where I was until night.

The thirty-eight foot cruiser became a white dot in the distance and disappeared. The channel was filled with boats now, outboard powered rowboats, sea skiffs, cabin cruisers, sailboats. There was even one ketch-rigged sloop beating south. It looked like a scene on a picture postcard. The kind the tourists send home.

I sorted the buildings on the mainland until I located Cliffton's store. It wasn't difficult to find. A half dozen of the hotels and as many office buildings were twice as tall. But Cliffton's was white, a block square, four stories high, with a big flag whipping atop a slim pole.

I visualized the man as I remembered him. He was a dapper little man with widespread alert eyes. I'd never seen him in repose. He was always on the go, thinking, scheming, planning. As far as I knew he'd never married, although scuttlebutt along the waterfront had established him as something of a stud. If so, he was probably as good at it as he was at everything else.

Now Cliffton wanted to marry Beth. He'd advised her to divorce me and marry him. He'd offered to buy the island. I knew why he wanted to marry Beth. She was lovely. For the past four years she'd been alone. It could be that he'd been getting samples. The more I thought about it, the more certain I was someone had. Beth had changed. But why did Cliffton want to buy the island?

I took off the gabardine shirt and kneaded sweat into my sore shoulder muscles. I wondered how I could have been so blind so long. I'd asked Beth what Cliffton's reaction was going to be when she told him she'd talked to me. I'd warned her that

77

he'd probably reach for his phone and call Ken. That was probably what was happening right now.

Beth had slipped right there. She'd called him by his first name. Then she'd corrected herself. She's said, *"You're doing Joe, Mr. Cliffton, a big injustice, Charlie. He's really a very fine and honorable man. You might as well accuse him of being Señor Peso as being capable of doing such a thing as you've just said."*

Well, why not? I should have thought of him in the first place. Men of his type lived to make money. They never had enough. He could well be *Señor Peso.* The more I thought of it the more logical it seemed. He'd built his business on cut prices. He had a store that sold everything from perfume to watches, from guava jelly to drugs, from imported cigars to the best in whiskies and wines. He had a Cuban agent in Habana. I knew that. I remembered hearing Beth say so. More, he had the merchandising connections in the States to get rid of anything too hot for him to handle.

Cliffton had known that I'd been having trouble meeting the payments on my boat. He'd known Beth had had a miscarriage. What would have been simpler than for him to pick up his phone and call me.

"This is Señor Peso, Captain White. How would you like to make two thousand dollars?"

Then, when he had decided that Beth was more valuable to him than I was, all he'd had to do was pick up his phone again and tip the Coast Guard.

How dumb could a man be? I wanted to talk to Mr. Cliffton. If I weren't picked up and jugged before I could.

I dropped back into the attic and found the sneakers I'd remembered. Beth had saved them. She'd also saved an old pair of dungarees, a blue chambray shirt, and one of my old white caps. I put them on and felt like myself again.

I walked down to the kitchen. One thing we'd forgotten was food. There was a can of beans in the pantry. That was all. I took them back to the captain's walk and ate them with my knife, watching the channel and the mainland. The beans tasted good.

Around eleven o'clock there was a stir of movement in Bill's boat basin. Also in the Coast Guard base on the point. A few minutes later, a cabin cruiser put out from the basin. It was joined in mid-channel by a Coast Guard boat.

I closed the trap and went downstairs. Then, wrapping the bean can in the shirt and pants I'd discarded, I walked outside and down the beach. From behind a tangle of mangrove trees, I watched the approaching boats.

Frenchy Gorman was running the cruiser. I'd fished as his partner lots of times. From the expression on Frenchy's face, I gathered his boat had been requisitioned. As far as he personally was concerned, he hoped they never found me. So I'd killed a woman. So what? A lot of women needed killing. He swung his boat alongside the shelf, cut his motor and dropped his anchor. Then he sat down on his bait box and rolled a cigarette.

Their faces red with the heat, their shirts already stained with sweat, Ken and Sergeant Strawn and a half-dozen uniformed Palmetto City patrolmen scrambled over the side and waded ashore in water up to their knees. An efficient young lieutenant j.g. followed them ashore from the Coast Guard boat. Four unenthusiastic enlisted men in fatigues came after him.

Ken was beginning to age. He was no longer just plump. He was beginning to look gross. There were dark bags under his eyes and indulgence lines in his face that hadn't been there four years before. I was glad I hadn't gone to see him before I talked to Beth. Ken was not my friend anymore. He was just another cop. A cop who looked like a preacher. A renegade preacher who liked his whiskey and women.

I felt a little sick just looking at him. Remembering. Remembering he'd been in love with Beth as long as I had, that Beth had made her choice between us. And I'd left Beth wide open when I'd gotten tied up with *Señor Peso* and Zo, and been sent away for four years.

Was it Ken? Was it Cliffton? Who? I had no right to be jealous. I was. While I'd been tucked away in a cell, someone had had a lot of fun teaching Beth the new tricks she had learned.

Ken and Strawn and the lieutenant j.g. walked up the stairs and into the house. The cops and the enlisted men squatted on the sand. Frenchy lighted his cigarette. I stood sweating, waiting. Five minutes passed. Then the three men came out.

The lieutenant j.g. admitted the obvious. "Someone's been here all right. And someone's been using that attic. Could be kids. Could be someone else." He looked at Ken. "Who did you say owns the old house, lieutenant?"

Gilly said, "Charlie White. The guy we're looking for."

The lieutenant j.g. wiped the sweat band of his cap. "Well, we'll keep a little closer watch on the island from now on. In fact, we'll swing around it right now. But outside of those cots in the attic, I don't see any sign that the house has been used

79

as a port of illegal entry. We'd have to have more than a few cots on which to base an official investigation."

It was the old game of passing the buck. The future admiral was good at it.

"As far as White is concerned, you want him. We don't. Until he breaks some federal law that comes under our jurisdiction, we haven't any interest in him. So I guess that bows us out."

He waded back to his boat. The enlisted men followed him, relieved.

Ken scratched his fat rear end. "The educated son of a bitch." He shrugged. "But I agree with him that a few cots in an attic don't mean anything. I think them high school kids have been holding parties out here."

One of the patrolmen said, "Boy. Would I like to go to one of them parties."

Ken gave him a sour look. "Well, let's get it over." He looked at the tangle of vegetation back of the house and along the shore without enthusiasm. "Fan out and we'll walk across it. You stay here, Scott, in case Charlie is still on the island and should try to double back."

One of the patrolmen got to his feet and walked up in the shade of the porch. "Yes, sir," he acknowledged.

Ken placed his men. "You take the left flank, Bill. Keep pretty well to the shore line. You do the same on the right, Pete. I'll take the middle. You other guys bird-dog between us." Ken's face got even redder. "This is a lot of crap as far as I'm concerned. Eight guys to search five hundred acres. But the chief says we search so we search."

He was wearing his gun stuffed into the tight waist band of his trousers. He tugged it out and broke it. There was no shell under the hammer. He thumbed a shell into the empty chamber. "If you should see White, don't take any chances. Shoot. You fellows understand that?"

The men said, "Yes, sir," soberly, in unison.

I moved back from the tangle of mangrove and faded into the thicker vegetation, being careful not to step on anything brittle. The heavy summer rains helped me. But it wasn't going to be as easy as I had thought. Sweat dripped from my face, ran down my legs. The three or four really safe hiding places I'd had in mind were out. Ken wanted me—dead. And Ken knew the island almost as well as I did. Ken had been born on it, too. On the far side. In a squatter's shack on one of the coves.

I walked faster, ducking under low-hanging branches, sucking in my guts as I slipped past wild lemon trees, hung with knobby lemons as big as footballs and studded with inch-long thorns. I realized I was still carrying the rolled up pants and shirt and bean can. I burrowed a hole in a pile of leaves, buried the bundle and walked on.

There was or had been a small five-acre cypress swamp in the middle of the island. It was, as I remembered, surrounded by a savannah of tall grass. At this time of the year, both the savannah and the swamp should be filled with water. It wasn't one of the hiding places I'd planned. But if I could reach the swamp, the only way they could flush me out, would be to bring one or more small boats to the island. By the time they could return with a boat it would be night. I angled toward the swamp.

The thrashing in the scrub behind me grew louder. "Charlie," Ken called softly. "Charlie."

There was a lulling, soothing quality to his voice. It was as if the one word meant much, meant: *"This is your old friend, Ken. Don't be afraid. Trust me. I want to help you, Charlie."*

It was darker here. The trees were thicker, their branches laced over my head. There was less underbrush. I stepped back of a tree and waited until I could see Ken in the small clearing I'd just raced across.

He'd outdistanced the man on either side of him by three hundred yards. His face was scarlet with exertion as he walked with the light fast tread some fat men have. His soft hat was tugged over his eyes to shield them. He was holding his gun shoulder high, the muzzle tilted. As I watched, he stopped and called again.

"Charlie. I know you're in here. Answer me."

There was the same lying smile in his voice as he paused with his gun barrel lifted. He waited licking his thick lips. His grey eyes darted from side to side.

The sweat draining down my spine turned cold. For some reason Ken hated my guts. He wanted to kill me. Personally. Why? Because he was a cop? Because he had a guilty conscience? Because he'd been two-timing me with Beth?

He called a third time, "Answer me, Charlie. I want to help you."

I thought, "You lying fat cracker," and slipped on to the next tree. I could see the saw-grass now. The water was knee-deep. I waded out into the grass trying to keep from splashing and went through the grass to the swamp. There was a deep hole in the far side of the grass. I forgot it and went under. I broke water spitting and clawing at a thick cypress root. The root lifted its head and opened its mouth at me. Its mouth was a dirty cotton

81

some ruddy, horny-handed men who looked like outdoors laborers. There were butchers, bakers and bookmakers. There were dressy men and men in cloth caps with colored kerchiefs tied round their necks.

Doug Savage, pot-landlord of the Prodigal Son Inn, was there, Laurie Lovett was there, and so was Clogger Roach. Three inveterate gamblers.

In the middle of the ring a fresh-faced young fellow was saying: "I'll head 'em for four," and there were four one-pound notes in the hands of the sturdy, red-faced man who stood beside him.

"Has he done it twice?" Bill Bragg inquired, and the reply was an envious "That's right, chum," from a shabby, gaunt, colorless man who looked as if he ought to be spending his cash-in-hand on a good meal. Evidently the challenger had started with a one-pound bet. He had won twice, leaving stakes and winnings in the ring.

"I'll have a nicker on," said Bill, making up his mind quickly, and feeling proudly resolute because he had done so. He handed a note to the red-faced man, who took it and nodded in acknowledgment. The colorless man, after a moment of obviously painful indecision, risked a pound himself. Then Lolly Jakes and Doug Savage stepped forward together, each offering two pounds to the stakeholder.

The stakeholder, whose remuneration largely depended upon tips from the day's winners, wanted to make no enemies. "Now then," he said with a dry grin. "Whose money shall I take?"

"I was first," said Doug.

"Nay, I'm damned if you were," Lolly retorted.

The two men eyed each other; measured each other. They were both burly men; the innkeeper clean and almost dapper in appearance, the other carelessly dressed. The onlookers watched them with interest.

Nearly all gamblers have ideas about the fickleness of luck. Any small incident might affect luck or point the way to the' avoidance of misfortune. And one lucky bet might change the whole day's fortunes. Therefore it became important to both Doug and Lolly that they should make that particular bet. It seemed to each of them that the other was blocking his way to an important initial success.

"Split it. Have a quid apiece on," the stakeholder suggested.

"Fair enough," Lolly agreed.

"I was first," said Doug stubbornly.

"Spin a coin for it," somebody advised.

The disputants shook their heads. Such a course might put a hoodoo on the bet.

82

NIGHT WAS LONG in coming. When it did come, I crawled out of the swamp and made my way, cautiously, back to the shore. No one tried to stop me. No one stepped out from behind a tree. Frenchy's boat was gone. I watched the house for a long time. There was no giveaway glow of a cigar or cigarette tip.

I was tired. I was hungry. My arms and shoulders were on fire with insect bites. Time was when sand flies and mosquitoes didn't bother me. After four years in a cell, I'd lost my immunity. The bugs had been bad during the day. With night they had become unbearable. I chewed a wet cigarette, wishing I had a dry smoke.

The tide was at full ebb but starting to come in. I waded out to the edge of the shelf and, squatting in the saw grass, I rubbed salt water and wet sand on the bites. It helped some, but not much.

I walked to the house and sat on the steps. I'd been all right while it was still daylight. Now I was beginning to panic, to start at sounds. I wasn't afraid of the dark. I was afraid of what might come out of it.

Hiding on the island had become like hiding in a fish bowl. The wetbacks in the attic hadn't gotten there by themselves. Someone had brought them to the island. Someone had taken them off. That someone knew I had seen them.

Then there was Ken. Ken knew I was on the island. Alone. For some reason Ken hated me. For some reason he'd made the manhunt personal. Was it because of Beth? Or was there another reason? But of one thing I was sure . . . Ken wanted to empty his gun in my guts!

I thought of the white cap bobbing on the pool and shuddered. My head ached. I was confused. I wished I was smarter than I was. Beth had promised to come out tonight or tomorrow night at the latest. I couldn't let her come to the island. I had to warn her somehow. I had to get off the island myself before the moon rose. But where to go?

The sound of tolling church bells on the mainland reminded me it was Sunday night. Outside of the drone of the mosquitoes and the gentle lapping of the tide, the night was a great black vacuum, filled only with the far-off tolling of the bells. Tolling for me. Tolling for Zo.

"I love you, Captain Charlie."

How long ago had Zo died? How long had I been running? It seemed that I'd been running all my life. I'd never felt so sorry for myself. A man made one mistake. And he paid. He paid for it all his life. Until he was dead.

If I hadn't listened to *Señor Peso*, I could be going to church tonight. I could be sitting beside Beth, listening to Reverend Paul. After church, we could stop in at the drugstore for a cup of coffee and a sandwich. We could laugh and kid a bit with other couples. We could walk home together openly. We wouldn't need to hide in darkness. I could watch Beth undress. We could go to bed together. I wouldn't have to wonder who'd been the other man in her life. I could get up in the morning and go out to the snapper banks, or take out a deep sea charter party, or—

I stopped it there. With the tolling of the bells I was thinking a lot of crap. A man was what he was. Like he either drank or he didn't. If I could, I wouldn't go to church. I wouldn't stop for coffee and sandwiches on our way home. I'd be more apt to stop in at the Jockey Club bar or at Sally's. Beth would look primly disapproving while I washed down a few shots with beers. And when we got home, we'd argue. What did I think this was, Tuesday night?

If it hadn't been for the phone call from *Señor Peso*, it would have been something else. Sure I'd needed the money. But after that first scared trip, when I'd met the *Andros Ancropolis* eighty miles out in the gulf, when I'd realized what I was in, I'd gotten as big a kick out of the excitement as I had out of the money. I was, it would seem, a born bastard. What I needed right now, was more of what I'd had the night before, a three-inch steak and about a half a fifth of rum. Zo had summed it up when I'd told her I was going back to Palmetto City to sell real estate or something. All she had said was:

"I laugh."

The mosquitoes and sand flies were making the steps unbearable. I searched the channel for the running light of a boat. There wasn't any. I got up and went into the house. The rusted screens would be some protection. I might even find a cigarette butt I could smoke. If I could find a match to light it.

84

The house was darker than the night. I started back toward the kitchen, stopped as a floor board squeaked. Then I twisted frantically to one side and flung myself forward, rolling, as a shot rattled the windows of the living room. Bullets followed me as I rolled, pecking at the floor boards behind me like so many angry redheaded woodpeckers tracking down an elusive worm.

The first shot burned across my ribs. The others had come close, but not quite close enough. I lay at the end of my roll, holding my breath, waiting for Ken to speak.

A moment of deep silence followed. Somewhere on the mainland a belated church bell began to toll after the others had stopped. Then I heard hoarse, subdued breathing and a stealthy snick of metal as the man who had fired attempted to slip the clip from his gun and insert a new one without me hearing him.

It was like hitting a wall head on. He grunted and dropped one of the clips he was handling. From the thud it sounded like the full one. Then he reversed the gun and tried to use it as a club.

I crowded him still closer, beating at his ribs and kidneys. He whimpered and gave ground, but continued to flail at me with the gun. A blow to the back of my ear dropped me. As I went to my knees, I wrapped my arms around his legs and heaved him over my back. A bone snapped as he landed. He screamed and clawed his way across the floor away from me. I followed him on my knees, feeling for him in the dark.

He screamed again and kicked at me. His shoe landed low on my chest. Then he was on his feet again and above me, racing up the stairs. I clawed after him. On the top stair, he turned and kicked again, more of a thrust of his leg than a kick. I caught at his ankle as I fell and he went over my head again. I fell grabbing for the rail with my left hand.

Both of us were cursing. I caught the rail. It swung me around with my back to the hard wood spindles. With such force, the spindles cracked and I went through them. He landed somewhere below me in the darkness and stopped cursing.

My backside pushed through the spindles like a yard baby stuck on his potty. I clung to the rail gasping for breath, blood mixed with sweat on my face. Then I pulled myself back on the stairs.

The lad at the foot of the stairs hadn't moved since he landed. I felt my way down a step at a time toward the sprawled blob of deeper black. Trying to save himself, he had turned in mid-air and landed on his back. I stepped over his legs, felt the palm of

85

a hand under the heel of my sneaker and stomped it hard before the fingers could close.

"You son of a bitch."

The hand rocked under my heel. He continued to lie motionless, silent. Still panting, I knelt beside him and patted his pockets for matches. There was a book in his shirt pocket. I wanted to find the gun and the full clip before he came to. I struck a match and turned. Then very quickly I turned back again.

The man on the floor wasn't Ken. It was the big lad who'd tried to knife me in the alley behind Beth's apartment. I studied his face, the match rising and falling with my breathing until it burned my fingers. I dropped it and lit another.

His face was in no way familiar. He was wearing blue slacks and thick-soled sneakers and a blue sports shirt. There was a pack of cigarettes in one of his shirt pockets. I slipped it out and touched the match to one of them. Then I dropped the pack in my own pocket. He didn't need it any more. He'd quit smoking. Suddenly. When the back of his neck made contact with the riser of the first step.

I found the gun and the full clip he'd dropped. Then I walked back and, squatting beside him again, I went through his pockets carefully. They didn't tell me any more than his face. All I found was another clip of shells to fit the gun, thirty-five dollars in bills and a small handful of silver. I gave him back the bills and silver and kept the clip. Then I went out into the kitchen and washed.

The hand pump on the sink was still in prime. I filled the sink with water and bathed my face and head. The water was lukewarm and smelled of sulphur, but it was better than what I had on my face. Finished, I used the tail of my shirt as a towel and walked back and looked at the dead man.

I wished I knew who the bastard was and why he'd wanted to kill me; who had sent him to kill me.

A touch of silver crossed the doorway. The moon was beginning to rise. I snuffed my cigarette and went out on the porch. More time had elapsed than I'd realized. I limped down the weed grown path to the shore.

The voice came off the water—faintly.

"Ahoy, the island, Charlie."

Just the four words. No more. A full minute of silence followed. Then I heard the muffled snort of an underwater exhaust and the sound of an idled marine motor. Whoever it was, was running without lights, not very far off shore. The voice came again. Slightly louder this time.

86

"Ahoy, the island. Charlie."

I waded out onto the flat, keeping well in the shadows of the mangroves and squatted down, straining my eyes to see the craft. It glided by, fifty feet off shore and I recognized the silhouette of Frenchy Gorman's thirty footer.

Frenchy's eyes were as good as mine. The idling screw reversed. The snortle of the exhaust became more pronounced. His voice was a low-pitched whisper. "That you squatting in them shallows, Charlie?"

I debated a moment before I answered. "Yeah."

Frenchy sounded relieved. "Good. I most give you out. I been cruising this goddam island since dusk-dark."

I took the gun from my pocket and slipped the safety. "You alone?"

Frenchy sounded hurt. "You think I'd call out if I wasn't?"

I was still breathing hard from what had happened at the house. Washing my face had been a waste of time. The cuts on my face were still bleeding. I doubted I'd ever stop sweating. Until I was like the guy in the parlor. Like Swede. Still, if I could trust anyone beside Beth, I could trust Frenchy. "No," I admitted. "I don't."

I put the gun back in my pocket and stood up.

He called softly, "Then come aboard. You'd better swim out. I don't want to make any more noise than I have to."

I stepped off the shelf into deep water and swam out to the cruiser. Still keeping his voice down to a whisper Frenchy added, "There's a line hanging over the stern."

I found the rope and muscled myself up over the fish box into the open cockpit. It felt good to be on a boat again. I wished I was on one of my own. A hundred miles out in the Gulf. With its nose pointed at the Dry Tortugas and points south. With Beth in the galley getting supper.

Frenchy hadn't changed. He still smelled of good rum and cheap tobacco. A bald little man in his middle forties, with a wisp of black mustache etched in the saddle leather of his face, under perpetually twinkling black eyes and a hooked nose, he got a big bang out of life. He was a good fisherman. He was also a good friend. If he liked you, you could do no wrong. If he didn't like you, you were a no-good Yankee bastard. No matter where you were born. Surprisingly, nine times out of ten he was right.

I tried to control my breathing. "How did you know I was on the island?"

He showed me his white teeth. They were all I could see of his face. "I seen you."

"When?"

Frenchy was amused. "This morning."

"This morning?"

"Yeah. When I brought Strawn and Gilly out. You were standing down the shore, say maybe two hundred feet from the path. Back of some mangrove. With a bundle under your arm."

"That's right."

"You're damn right that's right."

"Why didn't you tell Ken?"

Frenchy spat over the side of the boat and took his makings from his pocket. "That no good Yankee-bastid." He spilled tobacco in a paper. " 'Run me out to the island,' he says. 'Police business.' "

I felt my way. "Ken's a cop."

"So what?"

I didn't say anything. I couldn't. I'd reached the end of my rope. The lights on the mainland were revolving slowly. My knees began to shake. I tried to stop them by bracing my feet. It didn't help. My whole body began to shake.

His back to the mainland, Frenchy lighted a match to touch off his cigarette, the flame cupped in his palms. He saw my face. He exhaled slowly. "Cripes. What happened to you, Charlie?"

I told him. Through chattering teeth. "I just killed a man."

"In a fight?"

"Yeah."

"Why?"

"Because he tried to kill me."

"Where?"

"In the house."

"Who?"

"I don't know. I don't know who he is. I only saw him once before. Last night. When he tried to knife me outside of Beth's apartment."

"Was he alone?"

"I don't know that, either."

Frenchy pinched his hooked nose in deep thought. "Well, in that case," he decided, as he reversed the screw and swung the cruiser in a wide arch away from the shore, "Maybe we better get out of here."

CHAPTER SIXTEEN

As WE SWUNG OUT away from the shelf, still running without lights, Frenchy reached in the wheel locker and handed me an unopened bottle of rum. "Get some of that in you before you try to talk anymore."

I peeled the plastic and pulled the cork with my teeth. The rum tasted good all the way down. When it reached my stomach, it spread out to my toes and fingers. I took another drink, the neck of the bottle clattering against my teeth. The shaking subsided gradually.

I corked the bottle and handed it back to Frenchy. He gave me a towel in exchange. "Now peel off those wet things. There's some dry pants and a shirt on my bunk. Also a cap and some sneakers. No thanks to me. Your missus brought 'em."

I caught his arm. "Beth sent you out to the island?"

"That's right."

"Why?"

"Because she's been nearly nuts all day, worrying about you. She came down to the basin right after I brought Gilly and Sergeant Strawn back, and them other dumb cops. She was going to rent a kicker from Frazer and go out, but she was afraid the cops were watching her. They were, too. It would have been a dead giveaway. Gilly made all the bait camp boys agree to keep a record of who they rented boats and kickers to today. They done it, too." Frenchy didn't like bait camp men on general principles. "Names and addresses. Just like he asked. Goddamn no-good-Yankee-bastids."

I stripped and toweled till I glowed. "Gilly isn't so dumb. He knew I was on the island."

"That ain't what he's saying along the water."

"What is he saying?"

"That you're probably on your way to Cuba."

"Ken hates my guts."

"That's why your missus was so worried."

89

I asked him flatly, "Why?"

Frenchy leaned out to make certain he was clearing the number six bouy. "She told me this afternoon. Ken's been after her ever since you got sent up. He wanted her to divorce you and marry him."

That made two of them. I stepped down into the cabin. There was a pair of socks and shorts and a tee shirt with the shirts and pants. All of them were new. In a Cliffton bag.

Frenchy gunned his engine a little. "As Beth told it he damn near went nuts when she'd told him she'd written you a letter saying she was willing to start all over. They had her down at the station two hours this morning trying to make her admit that you were in her apartment when Gilly and Strawn banged the door last night."

The cap fitted as well as the rest of the clothes. I stepped up into the cockpit again and nonchalantly leaned against the live-bait well. "How come, Frenchy?"

He knew what I meant. "Let's say you done me favors in the past."

"I'm awfully hot."

Frenchy wasn't perturbed. "You're telling me? I couldn't even get the baseball game today." He imitated a radio announcer. " 'Now Minoso is stepping up to the batter's box. Now Vic Raschi is winding up. Here comes the pitch. Minoso swings at it hard—and we interrupt this broadcast to tell you that Charlie White, the ex-convict who is the object of the most intense man-hunt this state has ever seen has just been spotted in a black Chevrolet coupe on Clearwater Causeway, drinking in the Tampa Terrace, picking up shell on Anna Maria beach, eating at a hot dog stand in Sarasota! Believe me, Charlie. That goddamn no-good-Yankee-bastid may have known you were on the island. But you're driving the rest of the state nuts."

The cigarettes I'd taken off the dead man had gotten soaked swimming out to the boat. I borrowed Frenchy's makings and rolled a cigarette. "Okay. Go ahead and ask me."

"Ast you what?"

"Did I kill Zo?"

Frenchy idled his engine, barely maintaining seaway, letting the sweep of the incoming tide carry us past the boat basin, the string of bait camps and the Coast Guard base on the point. "Okay. Did you kill Zo?"

"No."

"I figured that," Frenchy said. "You know who did?"

"No."

He inclined his head at the island now lying astern. "How about this guy you told me about?"

"I don't know. I doubt it."

"Why?"

"It's just a feeling."

"What kind of a feeling?"

"That he was only a hired hand." I lighted the cigarette I'd rolled. "Who's running wetbacks, Frenchy?"

Frenchy was silent a long time. "That," he said, finally, "is something I don't know. And I'm not holding out. I've heard rumors from time to time. But never pinned on no one guy. You know how it is along the water."

"Yeah. I know."

"Then it's true about them cots in the attic?"

"Yeah. There was a dozen guys in it this morning. They jumped me when I opened the door. When I came to, I was under the house. The way I figure it, Ken and Strawn and that Coast Guard j.g. showing up to search the house was all that saved me. Whoever parked the merchandise didn't have time to kill me. They had to get their cattle off the island. They took them off the back way. Which one of the boys has a new thirty-eight foot, double cabin, twin screw with a flying bridge? Painted white?"

Past the point and the Number One light, Frenchy gunned his engine and relaxed on the stool. "There's only one boat around here that answers that description."

"Who owns it?"

"Who do you think? Cliffton."

I found the rum bottle and uncorked it and let the rum trickle down my throat, enjoying the taste. What Frenchy had just told me tied in with what I'd figured. With me tucked away so he could make his play for Beth, Cliffton would need a boat and someone to replace me. The rum on an empty stomach was making me light-headed. I'd need all the brains I had. I corked the bottle and put it back in the locker.

"Who's running it for Cliffton?"

"Matt Heely."

"What happened to Matt's boat?"

"He got drunk with the charter party he had aboard the last night of the tarpon round-up four years ago. Right after you were sent away. And coming back just before dawn in a fog, he missed the goddamn channel lights by sixty feet and piled up on the breakwater. Damn near drowned all his sports. From what I hear, they're still suing him for this and that."

91

The picture was familiar. A guy pacing the floor at night. Desperate. In a tight spot for money. All he knows is the water. The phone rings.

"This is Señor Peso, Captain Heely. How would you like to have a good job? One that will pay you real money? Put a wheel in your hands again?"

So what should the guy say? "No?"

Only Matt was in deeper than I'd been. If Matt were running Cliffton's boat, he knew who *Señor Peso* was.

"Why?" Frenchy asked. "You see Cliffton's boat this morning?"

"Or one just like it. Pulling out of one of the coves on the far side of the island. While Ken and Strawn were pulling up in front."

Frenchy took the bottle from the locker, took a big drink, held it up to the rising moon, then passed it on to me. "Kill it and bust the bottle. There's no stamp on it."

I killed it and smashed it on the rail and dropped the pieces over the side. It didn't set as well as the first drink I'd taken. I was suddenly sick of the whole mess. So Cliffton was *Señor Peso?* All I wanted was out. I wasn't mad at anybody. Not even Ken. With forty-eight thousand dollars, Beth and I could start all over again. I'd be any kind of a husband she wanted me to be. *If* I could get out.

I was almost afraid to ask. "Where are we headed now?"

"Across the bay to Sally's."

"Beth is waiting for me there?"

Frenchy nodded. "Yeah. I ran her over before I started looking for you. I figured if we were ordered to heave-to, you could go over the side. She couldn't."

I said, "Sally's is a hell of a place for her to be."

Frenchy got a little sore. "Where do you expect her to meet you? On the steps of the city hall? Or in front of the band shell in Phillips Park? As you remarked before, you are a little warm."

"Yeah. That's right," I admitted.

Few folks except commercial fishermen and guides even know about Sally's. There is a road of sorts, across the flats, but no one ever uses it. Not even delivery trucks. Sally brings in his own supplies by boat. Those he buys in Tampa or Palmetto City. The rest are dropped off in the dark of the moon. A big Portugee weighing three hundred pounds, Salvatore caters to an exclusive clientele. The bar and hotel are built on pilings at the end of a series of inlets and swash channels. It takes a guide who knows that particular section of water to navigate it. He serves good drinks and good food. There is gambling of course. And if a drunken commercial fisherman with a thousand pounds of pompano burning a hole in his pocket should happen to require feminine companionship, Sally's waitresses double in brass. For a price.

Contacting Matt Heely was out. I was glad I hadn't suggested it to Beth. If Matt were working for Cliffton and Cliffton were *Señor Peso*, Matt would probably have agreed to run me anywhere I wanted to go. Then dropped me off in forty-fathoms. With an anchor tied to my ankles.

I took off my cap and let the wind blow through my hair, relaxed for the first time in two days.

I thought it over, then asked it. "How's for you running me and Beth to Cuba, Frenchy? I can make it worth your while. Enough to buy a new boat."

He sounded genuinely regretful. "Geez, I'd like to, Charlie. I could use a new boat. But—"

"But what?"

He thumped the side of his boat. "But we'd never make it in this tub. She's going to twist to pieces on me some night, sure. She's rotten from the bottom up. More, she's got so many worms in her they keep me awake nights, listening to them eat up my bread and butter."

"How about Fort Myers?"

"I could make it to Myers, I guess. Hell. I go out to the banks every day."

I said, "I could get either Skip or Harvey to run us on from there."

"Yeah. You probably could," Frenchy said. He was silent for a long time. Then he said, quietly, "But keeping on running ain't going to do you a damn bit of good, Charlie. Even if you get to Cuba."

"Why won't it?"

Frenchy took a fresh bottle of rum from the locker and cracked the seal. He took a big drink, then handed the bottle to me. "I been thinking about that, ever since they been hunting for you."

I wet my lips and stood holding the bottle.

"Why won't it?" I repeated.

Frenchy eased the boat up an unmarked swash channel into a dark inlet, lined on both sides with mangroves. "You ain't got a chance in Cuba, Charlie."

"Why haven't I?"

"What was the name of the girl you're accused of killing? Her right name."

"Zo Palmyra."

"She was an American national?"

"No. Zo was Cuban. I met her in Habana."

Frenchy cut his engine still more. We were barely creeping now. The mangrove was so close I could have reached out with a boat hook and touched it. "So there you are," he said.

I shook my head. "I don't get it."

He leaned still farther out of the boat, keeping his eyes on a feeble yellow glow winking through the mangrove. It was the low watt bulb on Sally's pier, powered by his own generating plant.

Frenchy said. "Use your head, Charlie. After all the stink there's been in the papers and over the radio, with your name and description and hers spread all over the state, and beamed to Cuba, you think the Cuban cops are going to let you hole up there?"

Some of the rum glow faded. We scraped on a bar, slid over it.

Frenchy continued. "You think they're going to let you walk down the Prado just like nothing has happened, maybe even give you a charter boat permit? The hell they will."

The dream began to fade.

Frenchy angled through another swash channel into deep water again and gunned his engine. "The hell they will," he repeated. "If you get picked up in Cuba, and you will, the chances are you won't even be extradited. They won't take any chance you might get free after killing one of their nationals. Cuban cops are the same as any other cops. They'll take care of the matter themselves. I can't say I blame them."

I gripped the rail of the boat and lost the rum I'd swilled on an empty stomach. Frenchy was right. All I'd been doing was kidding myself. Swede had been right about so many things. The days of sailing by guess and by God were gone. There were no safe ports for a man accused of murder. I could change my name. I could change my mannerisms. I could even change my means of livelihood. But I couldn't change my hair or my face or my body. Or the charge against me.

"Wanted for murder, Charles White, red-haired, freckles on face, six feet tall, two hundred pounds," meant just the same in Spanish as it did in English.

Forty-eight thousand dollars. That was a laugh. I didn't have a dime. The chances were I wouldn't last long enough to get

94

from the shore to the bank. The first Habana *policia* to see me would throw me in the jug. And cork it.

I began to shake again. The rum bottle dropped out of my hand into the boiling wake back of the screw.

It bobbed a moment. Then sank. I envied it.

CHAPTER SEVENTEEN

THERE WERE A HALF DOZEN boats made fast along the pier. All but one were commercial fishing boats. The exception was Cork Avers charter boat. I jumped up on the planking, caught the rope Frenchy threw me and dropped it over a piling. He made the stern fast and joined me.

The juke in the bar was blaring something about a moon. I asked Frenchy the name of the song.

He said, "I think it's *How High Is The Moon*. It came out since you've been away."

How high is the moon? How deep is down? Where did I go from here? The pier was long and narrow, with heaps of oyster and clam shells piled high on both sides. We walked back through the stink of the tide flats, the loose boards rattling under our feet.

The bar was sided with cypress slabs. Unpainted. Patched here and there with driftwood. With a crescent moon hovering over it, Sally's looked romantic. It wasn't. It was hot. Hot as only tide flats can be hot. It was dirty. It stank. The throb of the generator that supplied the electric power became a second pulse in the ears.

There were eight or nine men at the bar. All of them nodded at Frenchy. One or two said, "Hi."

None of them paid any attention to me. They weren't being unfriendly. They were minding their own business. It was the only house rule at Sally's.

A drunken little brunette, who was about to pop out of the bodice of her white off-the-shoulder blouse, was sitting at a table with Cork Avers. She managed to focus her eyes on me and

95

gasped, "Migawd! Ain't that Charlie White? Ain't that the guy they're looking for on the radio?"

"Shut your goddamn mouth," Cork told her. And went on beating time to the music with the bottom of a half-full bottle of Old Angus.

I'd never known Sally to wear shoes. He wasn't now. He was behind the wood, barefooted. With no shirt. Wearing a pair of white duck pants. His belly bulged over the turned down waist band. Sally was getting old. The mat of black hair on his chest was flecked with gray. His face wasn't fat. It was flabby. He'd made a lot of money. On the wrong side of the law. He'd earned it.

"Gentlemen," he said. He set two sweaty bottles of beer on the bar. Then barely glancing at me, he inclined his head at the door, leading back to the rooms he rented, and his lips formed the figure seven.

"How they going, Sally?" Frenchy asked him.

"Fine. Just fine," Sally replied.

I wet my lips with the beer. Then I walked back down the hall and ran my knuckles across the louvred door of Number 7.

Beth's voice sounded small and frightened. "Who is it?"

"Charlie."

She unlocked the door. I closed and locked it behind me. The room was small. Square. With unpainted pine walls. There was a chair, a table, a bed. To keep her dress from getting stained with perspiration, Beth had taken it off and hung it on a hanger on the wall. All she had on was a pale nylon slip and a pair of low-heeled white sandals. The heat in the box of a room had tightened her curls into wet little ringlets. Sweat plastered the sheer slip to her lovely body.

"I was afraid to wait outside," she said. "So Mr. Salvaterra rented me this room."

A naked twenty-five watt bulb hung from the ceiling on a green cord. I held her at arm's length and looked at her. She was as lovely as I remembered her. By moonlight. But Beth, too, had aged. There were faint lines in her face and deep purple shadows under her eyes.

I tilted her chin. "You look like a bride."

She stood on tiptoe and kissed me feverishly. "I feel like one." Then she buried her face on my new shirt and cried. "I've been so worried."

I held her tight against me for a moment. Her body was sweet in my arms. Then she looked up again and touched the

96

cuts and contusions on my face with the tips of her fingers. "Who hurt you?"

I said, "You wouldn't know the guy. It was a fellow out on the island."

"Who?"

"I never saw him before."

"Where is he now?"

"He's dead."

"Who killed him?"

"I did."

Beth began to cry again, holding her head back, looking at me through tears. "What have we gotten into?"

I told her. "Even more of a mess than the Zo business. Someone's been using the old house as a drop for wetbacks."

"Wetbacks?"

"Smuggled aliens."

Her voice was no longer small. It was fierce. "Who?"

My knees were still shaky. I patted her heinie and sat on the chair. "We'll come to that." There was a pack of cigarettes on the table. I lighted one and sucked the smoke into my lungs. It was mental. But it made me think I felt better. "But first, I have to have some food."

"You haven't eaten?"

"Only a can of beans."

I unlocked the door and walked down the hall. Sally came to the end of the bar and raised one bushy eyebrow. I asked him what he had to eat. He said he could fix me almost anything. I settled on fresh smoked mullet, some cold hush puppies and some beer.

Beth was sitting on the bed when I got back. I put the tray on the table and locked the door again. She talked as I wolfed the fish. "I talked to Mr. Cliffton today. And you were right about him. He laughed at me. He said there wasn't the least doubt that you'd killed Zo and that spending money on a private detective would be foolish."

I said, "We'll come to Cliffton. Right now, let's talk about Ken."

"What about him?"

"He came out to the island twice."

"I know. That's why I was so worried."

"What's more, he knew I was there. He had me trapped in the swamp. But he didn't want me arrested. He wants to kill me. He tried to. Not because he's a cop. Because he hates my intestines. Why?"

Beth looked at the floor. Then ran the hem of her slip between her fingers. "Well, you know how it is with Ken. He's always been in love with me. I—I suppose he's jealous."

The mullet was good but greasy. The towel on the table was there for another purpose. I wiped my hands on it. "He has reason to be?"

Beth dropped her slip and raised her eyes to meet mine. "You've no right to ask me that."

The *thump thump—thump thump* of the power plant seemed to expand the heat in the room until the walls bulged. It was difficult for me to breathe. I washed down the mullet with a swig of beer. "I'm asking it, Beth."

"Even after Zo?"

"Yeah. Even after Zo."

Beth's lower lip quivered. Her mouth screwed up as if she were going to cry again. She lifted her hair up and away from the back of her neck, her pointed breasts rising with her arms. "All right, if you must know. Yes. He had."

The mullet didn't taste as good. I forced more down my throat. It stuck halfway.

A single tear rolled down Beth's cheek. Her eyes continued to meet mine. "I could stand you being sent to prison. I could stand you disgracing me. But the thought of you having another woman was more than I could take. Ken was good to me. He used to come out to the house after you were sent away, then up to the apartment. And just talk." A note of hysteria crept into her voice. "Then one night—it happened. I didn't care. At the time I was glad. I was getting even with you." She ran her hands over her breasts. "I even liked it. For the first time in my life, I liked it. It was as if some wall inside me had broken." More tears rolled down her cheeks. "That went on for about a month. Then I came to my senses. I realized what I was doing, how I was cheapening myself. I tried to stop it. I tried to break away from Ken." She sobbed hysterically. "But Ken wouldn't let me. He forced me to continue to have relations with him. He said he'd kill me if I didn't."

I got the morsel of mullet down. "The bastard." I was breathing as hard as she was. "The fat cracker bastard."

Beth continued to sob hysterically. "That's why he hates you. That's why he wants to kill you. He went crazy when I told him that I'd written you. That I'd sent you the fare to come to me. That I was going to start all over with you." She wiped her eyes with the back of her hand. "That's why I didn't write you a love letter. That's why I said we'd talk it over. I was going to tell

98

you everything. Then you showed up at the door and all that mattered was that you were with me again."

I walked over to the bed and sat beside her. "Beth, honey. Sweetheart."

Beth twisted out of my arms. "No. Don't touch me. It's all your fault that it happened. I'm not that sort of a person. I've been living a lie for four years." Sobs shook her body. "I've even been ashamed to go to church. I have to turn my head away when I see Reverend Paul on the street." She stood up and peeled off her slip. There was an ugly bruise on her stomach, another on her left breast. "If you don't believe me, look."

Her body was inches from mine. I panted. "Who beat you?"

She sobbed, "Ken. He came back to the apartment this morning. Alone." She screamed the words at me. "And he beat me because I wouldn't. Because I couldn't. Not after I'd been with you."

Beth flung herself face down on the bed, her shoulders heaving. I sat beside her, my heart pounding. Breathing hard. Drenched with sweat. Afraid to touch her. Afraid to try to comfort her. I'd done this to Beth. Me. Mr. Charles White. First class heel.

"I'll kill him," I panted. "I'll kill him."

Beth continued to cry. For a long time, the only sounds were the *thump thump—thump thump* of the power plant and her sobbing. Then Beth rolled over on her side and wiped her eyes with a lock of hair. "So now you know."

I nodded. "Yeah. So now I know." What could I say? That I was sorry?

She sniffed. "Light me a cigarette. Please."

I lighted one and gave it to her. Beth lay on her back sucking at it in the awkward, feverish way some women smoke. When she spoke her voice was small again.

"What are you going to do, Charlie? I mean about Ken?"

"Kill the bastard."

"And then?"

"I don't know."

"You hate me, don't you?"

I bent and kissed her, "Why should I hate you for something that was my fault? You talked to Cliffton?"

"Yes."

"Just what did he say?"

Beth brushed her hair out of her eyes. "Joe was horrid. He said there wasn't a doubt in his mind that you'd killed Zo. He said I was a fool to even give you a second thought."

99

"He knew you'd seen me?"

"No."

After what she'd just told me about Ken, it was a difficult question to ask. I picked up Beth's hand from the bed and played with it. "What about Cliffton, Beth?"

"What do you mean, what about Joe?"

"You call him Joe. You must know Mr. Cliffton pretty well."

Beth turned her face to the wall. "Why shouldn't I? I've been his confidential secretary for five years."

"How confidential?"

I turned her face back to mine. "How confidential?"

Beth's shoulders shook. She began to cry again. Silently. "You've no right to question me."

"You've stayed with him, too?"

Her lower lip quivered. "No."

"Don't lie to me."

"Well, once then."

My nerves were keying higher with every word she spoke. Like the E string of a violin. "Where?"

"On his boat."

"When?"

"About six months ago." Her lips twisted in revulsion. "Oh, not because I wanted to. He's been after me for years. In a very gentlemanly manner. Then this night on the boat he got drunk. Off Anna Maria."

"What were you doing on his boat?"

"He *said* he wanted me to take some important dictation. Oh, it was awful, Charlie. I tried to fight him off. But I couldn't. He carried me into his cabin and tore off my clothes and—and—" She couldn't go on.

I choked out the words. "It's happened since?"

"No."

"Why did you keep on working for him?"

"I had to eat. Besides, when Mr. Cliffton sobered up, he was as sorry it had happened as I was. He said it wouldn't have happened if he hadn't wanted and loved me for years. He begged me to divorce you and marry him. He said he'd give me the kind of a life and home that I deserved."

"Why didn't you marry him?"

Beth made a hopeless gesture with one hand. "I told you. I love you. Besides, I was all mixed up with Ken." She sobbed harder. Hysterically. "Oh, dear God. I wish I were dead."

I slapped her. Lightly. "Stop that." The *thump thump—thump thump* of the power plant was a bass drum in my ears. I realized

100

it wasn't the power plant. It was the pounding of my heart. I sounded like I was shouting at her. I was. "And stop blaming yourself. Everything that's happened is my fault. I exposed you to all of it by getting mixed up with *Señor Peso* and Zo in the first place. Cliffton has been persistent? I mean about you divorcing me and marrying him?"

"Very."

"It was Cliffton who suggested you move off the island?"

"Yes, I think it was."

"He knew you wrote me that letter?"

Beth rolled her head on the pillow. In torment. "I don't know. I don't know anything, Charlie. I'm not this sort of person. I don't want to be. All I know is that I want out of this trap. Why can't we go away somewhere? Anywhere. Away from here. Just so we're together."

The beer was lukewarm now, and sour. I rinsed my mouth with it and set the bottle back on the table. "Because we wouldn't get very far. Frenchy pointed that out on the way over here. I'd be arrested before I got to the bank in Habana."

"Then what are we going to do?"

I panted. "Have a show down. If I'm right, Cliffton is *Señor Peso.*"

Beth sat up on the bed and clung to me. She looked frightened. "You can prove it?"

"No," I admitted. "I can't. But it was Cliffton's boat that took those wetbacks off the island this morning. Cliffton has the connections to dispose of the stuff I brought in. He knew I needed money, needed it bad, four years ago. You say he's been after you for years. It was Cliffton who suggested that you move off the island."

Beth put the back of one hand to her forehead. "Of course. I should have realized that. I can see it all now. So plainly. It was Cliffton who gave Zo that money to keep you from coming back to me. Then, when he learned that I'd written you, he was afraid you might come back anyway. So he killed Zo and tried to kill you. It was Joe Cliffton's face you saw. Don't you see? He had to kill Zo. She knew who he was."

"He was out of town that night?"

"He was. He said on a business trip." Beth's eyes narrowed slightly. "What are you going to do about it, Charlie?"

I took the gun I'd taken from the hood out on the island out of my pocket and looked at it. "I don't know," I admitted. "I don't know, sweetheart. My brains weren't made for this kind

101

of thinking. I'm just a dumb charter boat captain. I don't know what to do."

"I do," she said, quietly. Her eyes narrowed still more. There were glints of gold in them now. "I know just what we ought to do to get even with both Ken and Mr. Cliffton." She unbuttoned the top button of my shirt and twisted a tuft of hair into a little peak.

"What?"

Beth evaded the question. "Would you be willing to take a chance, a big chance, sweetheart? If we could go away together. Fix it so your name would be cleared first? Be happy?"

I panted. "You know I would."

Beth moved still closer to me and ran the tip of her tongue around my lips. "And you know now that I love *you?*" She unbuttoned another button of my shirt.

"Yeah. Sure."

"And you still love me?"

"I do."

She unbuttoned two more buttons and patted my chest, her eyes searching mine. "You mean that, Charlie? You really love me? In spite of what I told you? About Ken? About Mr. Cliffton?"

The heat in the room was physical, tangible substance. Covering us like a wool blanket. Making it almost impossible to breathe. I could smell the raw pine, smell her. I gasped, "I told you it wasn't your fault."

Beth's eyes narrowed to mere slits. She sucked in her breath and held it as she massaged the sweaty flesh on my stomach. "And you forgive me"

The E string was tuned to the snapping point. I swallowed. To relieve the pressure in my ears. "Of course. Come to the point, Beth. Tell me what you want me to do. What I can do."

"I'll tell you," she said. "In a minute." Her upper lip curled away from her teeth. "But first prove you forgive me."

Then the only sounds in the room were the *thump thump—thump thump* of the power plant, the pounding of my heart, as I proved that I forgave her.

CHAPTER EIGHTEEN

BETH RENTED THE CAR. In her name. From the U-Drive-It firm near the basin. Frenchy stayed with me, talking in whispers, until Beth drove up to the tall royal palms under which we'd agreed to meet. Then Frenchy gripped my hand for luck and faded back into shadows. I got into the car with Beth.

It was a four door black Chevrolet.

Beth slid over as I got in. "You drive."

Rather than go around, I stepped over her legs and squeezed in back of the wheel. "What's the matter? Nervous?"

She bobbed her head. "I'll say." She opened her purse, took out a cigarette and lit it. "Look how my fingers are shaking."

I switched the ignition back on. "You're positive now you want to go through with this?"

Beth bobbed her head again. "It's the only possible way we can clear you, make things right for you and me again. You see that, don't you, Charlie?"

"Yeah. Sure." I agreed with her.

I started to let out the clutch. "No. Kiss me first," Beth insisted.

I kissed her. I felt good, and sad, at the same time. It was a funny feeling. I'd never had it before. It was as if I had died and come to life and was scheduled to die again at some specified time in the near future. And didn't give a damn.

As with most advice, Swede had been half right, half wrong. But he'd hit it on the head in at least one respect.

"A man hauls in the fish he baits for and at the level at which he fishes."

Beth was fiercely possessive. "Love me?"

"What do you think?" I asked her.

She smiled the self-satisfied little smile that women smile when they know they're sure of their men. "I know you do."

I eased the car into gear and drove slowly down the road rimming the waterfront. Clifton's sleek thirty-eight footer was in its slip. There was a light in the aft cabin. As we drove past, I could see Matt Heely propped up on one of the bunks, reading.

"Probably the Sunday comics," Beth said.

"Probably." I answered.

There were few cars on the road and fewer pedestrians on the walk. Phillips Park was deserted. So was downtown Palmetto City. But Cliffton's, when we reached it, was still open and crowded. At ten-thirty on a Sunday night. Cliffton's was always crowded. Seven days a week. From eight o'clock in the morning until midnight. Sunday was one of his big days. Most of the back country people came in then to do their shopping. Along with cut-rate prices, Cliffton always gave them a free show. One week it was a free circus in the parking lot. The next a troupe of hill-billy singers.

There was an empty place in the line of cars on the Fourteenth street side of the building, across from the Atlantic Coast Line depot. I backed into the space and started to get out.

"No," Beth stopped me. "Let me go in alone. It being late as it is, Joe may not be here. If not, we'll have to drive out to his house."

"And if he's here?"

"I'll get him out to the car somehow."

I asked her if she wanted a gun.

Beth was scornful. "I won't need a gun. Meanwhile, you be careful you're not recognized."

I promised I'd be careful. Beth kissed me again. Then she strode off down the walk, crisp and cool and lovely in a pastel green dress. Her yellow hair spun gold in the light from the big plate glass windows. Looking like a dewy-eyed vestal virgin. On her way to light a torch. After what had happened at Sally's.

Women.

I sat watching the crowd for a few minutes, then reached for a cigarette. I was out. Fresh out.

Hub Conners was directing traffic on the corner, but no one seemed to be watching the crowd. I slipped into the side door of Cliffton's and bought a pack of Camels. As I waited for my change, the public address system announced the last special of the day would be a banana split for sixteen cents to the first hundred customers only.

The office was on a glassed-in mezzanine. As far as I could tell it was dark. I sifted the crowd with my eyes, looking for Beth, and saw her, finally, in one of the telephone booths. The girl back of the counter was trying to give me my change.

"Will there be anything else, sir?"

There was a stack of unsold Sunday papers near the counter. I told her to take out fifteen cents for a paper and walked back to the car. By tilting the paper sideways, I could read fairly well by the lights in the show windows.

I could see what Frenchy meant. According to that morning's headline, I was driving the cops nuts. Every crank in Florida had phoned in with information concerning me. I'd been seen in a dozen places, from Pensacola to Key West.

I read on down the story. The general public had been alerted to watch for me. I was known to be armed and dangerous. My description followed. I skipped it. I knew what I looked like. Of more interest was an item pertaining to Zo. Some bright boy in the state patrol lab had begun to wonder why her fingers were broken in the manner that they were and just what they had been clasping when they had been broken.

I turned the pages of the paper. Swede was on page four, in a one column two inch box. All it said about him was that Swen (Swede) Olson, former fishing guide and well-known West Coast Florida charter boat captain, had been executed, in the manner and at the time prescribed by law, for killing a prison guard during an abortive attempted prison break.

I wondered if Swede had met Zo by now. I hoped so. I was suddenly lonely. Lonelier than I'd ever been in my life.

I tossed the paper on the back seat of the car and smoked a cigarette while I waited for Beth. She came weaving swiftly through the crowd, looking as pretty coming toward me as she had walking away.

"Mr. Cliffton wasn't in the office."

"Oh."

"I could see it wasn't lighted. But I went upstairs to make certain. That's what took me so long."

I said, "I see."

Beth was breathing hard. As if she'd hurried. The emotional and physical strain was beginning to tell on her.

"So?"

"So now we drive out to his house," she said. "But stop at the apartment first. I want to pack a small bag. Just in case things go wrong."

"What if there's a stake-out?"

Beth shook her head. "There won't be."

"How do you know?"

"I know."

I didn't say anything. There didn't seem to be anything to say.

Beth added, "Ken thinks you're still out at the island."

I asked, "What do we do about Ken?"

Beth folded her hands in her lap. "That's—up to you. You know what he's done to me."

I circled the block her apartment was in. There didn't seem to be a stake-out. Beth got out the second time around and was waiting on the curb clutching a small overnight case when I came around again.

I asked her what was in it. She put the case between her feet. "Clothes," she said.

I hadn't any idea where Cliffton lived. Beth directed me to the house. It was in a swank section of town that was called Small Bayou. You have to have money to live there. But Cliffton's house was neither large nor pretentious. It was a low, rambling, hollow tile affair, set well back from the road at the end of a landscaped, winding drive.

Beth looked at the house, then at me. As if to say, "I could have lived here if I wanted to. If it hadn't been for you. See what I gave up for you, Charlie?"

I parked the car under the dangling feelers of a banyan tree and cut the lights. It was black under the tree and silent, except for the croak of the tree frogs and the humming drone of mosquitoes.

Beth sat breathing hard. "I'm frightened."

I gave her a chance to back out. "Now's the time to call this off. If you want to. I can always go down to the police station and surrender. Maybe I'm wrong. Maybe they'll believe my story."

Beth's fingers bit into my arm. "No. I won't let you do that. They won't believe you. They'll send you away from me again." Her voice was barely audible. "Besides—"

"Besides what?"

"There's Ken."

I could taste the smoked mullet. "Yeah. There's Ken."

I opened the door on my side. "Well, let's get it over with."

She got out on her side and joined me, still clutching the overnight bag. There was a light in the living room window. There was also a light in the room beyond it. I judged this room to be a bedroom or study. The rest of the house was dark. None of the blinds were drawn.

I'd been wrong about the size of the house. The living room was huge. There was no one in it. I looked in through the window of the room beyond it. I'd been right about it being a study. Still fully dressed, even to his coat, Cliffton was sitting at a big

106

desk comparing what seemed to be bills of lading with entries in a huge loose-leaf ledger.

Beth's fingers bit into my arm. "Please."

"Please what?"

"Please kiss me for luck."

I kissed her. For luck. Her lips were hot and feverish. Not with passion. With fear. Her body trembled in my arms. I crushed her to me for a moment. "You're certain you want to go through with this?"

She bobbed her head. "I am. But, please. Not so tight, Charlie."

"Why?"

"You're mussing my dress."

I released her and pressed my back against the house, beside the door. "Okay. Go ahead. Ring the bell."

Beth pushed the button, chimes rang somewhere inside the house. A moment later, brisk footsteps crossed the parquet floor and the overhead porch light came on.

"Oh," Cliffton said. "It's you. What brings you here, this time of night, Beth."

Beth lied, "I want to talk about Charlie."

I waited for the door to open. It didn't. Cliffton stood with the screen between them, making no effort to unhook it. "They've caught him?"

"No. Not yet," Beth said. "I hope they never do. Well, aren't you going to ask me in?"

"It's eleven o'clock, Beth."

"So what?"

"I'm alone in the house."

"I have to see you. Talk to you. Please, Joe."

From where I stood, it sounded as if Cliffton sighed. "I don't know whether I should or not, Beth. To be perfectly candid, I'm a little afraid of you."

Beth's lips twisted in a funny little smile. "Afraid of me?"

Cliffton had a crisp, staccato way of talking that matched his movements. "Afraid of my own reactions. So if it's about your husband, I'd rather you wouldn't come in. I'd like to help you. You know how I feel about you. But I'm really very busy, Beth. I might add, and a bit perturbed."

I watched Beth's breasts rise and fall. I imagined that Cliffton was watching them, too. Her voice had a certain quality to it that I'd never heard before. "You're perturbed about what?"

"I'd rather not say," Cliffton said. "And as far as White is concerned, as I told you this morning, I can't see that hiring a private agency man to snoop around would do a bit of good. I had a long talk with Lieutenant Gilly after I talked to you. And Gilly says there isn't a doubt that White killed that girl in Dead Man's Bay."

Beth ran her free hand over one of her breasts. "Perhaps Lieutenant Gilly isn't exactly impartial."

"Even so."

"Then you refuse to let me in?"

Time was running out on me. Fast. I'd waited as long as I could. I grasped the knob of the screen door and pulled. It opened with a rasp of metal pulling out of wood.

Cliffton was every inch as small and dapper as I remembered him, with widespread, intelligent eyes and hair so black it looked like it had been dyed. He backed slowly away from the door as I walked in with Beth crowding on my heels. He seemed more puzzled than frightened.

"Who are you?"

"You wouldn't know?"

He recognized me then. "Oh, yes. Of course. You're Charles White. You're the man for whom every law enforcement officer in Florida is looking."

He still wasn't frightened. He looked from me to Beth. "A rather shabby trick, my dear. What am I supposed to do now? How am I supposed to react? What do you want of me?"

I sat on the padded arm of an expensive overstuffed chair. "Beth tells me you're in love with her."

I expected him to deny it. He didn't. He met my eyes instead. "That's right. Have been for some years. In fact, I've suggested a dozen times that she divorce you and marry me."

"She also tells me you want to buy the old house."

"That also is correct."

"Why?"

"Why what?"

"Why do you want to buy it?"

He got a little hot. "I don't consider that any of your business." Cliffton backed toward a long console table and sat on the edge of it.

I played out the string, exactly as Beth had suggested. "I intend to make it my business. Did you use your boat this morning?"

He lighted a cigarette. "No."

"You didn't send Heely out to the island to pick up the covey of wetbacks you had hiding out in the attic before Lieutenant

108

Gilly and Sergeant Strawn happened on to them, searching the old house for me?"

He knew the meaning of the term. "You're out of your mind. No one would dare such a thing in Palmetto City."

I was holding the gun I'd taken in my right hand. I used my left to light a cigarette.

I pointed out, "Someone did."

His eyes were as black as his hair. They narrowed slightly as he asked, "You can prove this?"

"No," I admitted. "I can't. But they were there. I know. I happened in on them. They beat me half to death. The only thing that saved me was Gilly and Strawn showing up to search the island for me."

"Gilly and Strawn saw them?"

"No. Your boat took them off the other side of the island."

Cliffton looked at Beth. "You believe this, Beth?"

Beth's voice was as hot as her eyes. "I do. The old house is ideally situated for just such a nasty business. Charlie's been in prison. I haven't been out there for years. Not since you suggested I move into town. To be *closer* to my work. You send Matt to Cuba at least once a month. The way we see it, he brought them back and dropped them at the house. Later, one by one, they were landed on the mainland as tourists. And the law or no one else would ever be the wiser, unless one of them should be picked up accidentally." Tears streamed down Beth's cheeks. "It's been you. It's been you all the time."

Cliffton seemed sincerely puzzled. "It has been I who did what?"

Beth said, fiercely, "Who tempted Charlie in the first place. Who got him into running contraband." She was practically screaming now. "And then you had him sent to prison."

Cliffton ran a hand over his hair. "You're mad. You're out of your minds. Both of you." He opened the drawer of the console table. Casually. As if in search of a cigarette.

"I wouldn't if I were you," I warned him.

He dropped the gun back in the drawer and closed it.

"All right. I won't." He took a package of cigarettes from his pocket and lighted one. "Just what is it you want of me?"

I told him. "A confession."

Cliffton blew smoke at the ceiling. He still seemed more puzzled than frightened. "What do you want me to confess?"

Beth told him. "That you're *Señor Peso*. That you hired a knife man to try to kill Charlie this morning. That you either

109

killed or had someone kill that Cuban girl Charlie is accused of killing."

Cliffton's fingers shook slightly as he lifted his cigarette to his mouth again. "I seem to be a pretty vicious sort of person. Just what could I hope to gain?"

Beth knew the answer to that one, too. She told him.

"Me."

CHAPTER NINETEEN

CLIFFTON WAS SILENT a long time. Then, looking at me, he asked, "I don't suppose it would do much good for me to deny these allegations that your wife's just made?"

"No," I admitted. "It wouldn't."

"You think I'm the mysterious *Señor Peso* that you mentioned at your trial?"

"We both do," Beth said.

Cliffton looked at her thoughtfully. "I didn't quite expect this from you, Beth. I guess it goes to prove that one lives and learns." He looked at me again. "Just what is your case against me, White?"

I told the truth. "I haven't any. Nothing but seemingly well-founded suspicions and the fact that it was your boat that took the wetbacks off the island this morning."

He suggested, "Maybe Heely is *Señor Peso.*"

Beth's lips twisted in scorn. "Matt hasn't enough brains to be *Señor Peso.*"

"No," I agreed with her. "He hasn't. *Peso* has been smart. Damn smart. But he slipped up in killing Zo and trying to kill me."

Cliffton pursed his lips. "It is your contention, then, that you didn't kill this Zo Palmyra?"

"It is."

"You think I did?"

"I do."

"You saw me do it?"

110

"No. The face of the man who slugged me and killed Zo was just a blur."

"And my motive?"

I said, "Beth told you that. She was the one thing you couldn't get at a bargain. But you could buy me. And you did. You brought me. With a phone conversation. *This is Señor Peso, Captain White. How would you like to make two thousand dollars?*' And like a chump I fell for it. And made you and myself a lot of money until you tipped the Coast Guard and had me tucked away for four years. It was probably you who first sicked Zo on me. In Cuba. And it was you who sent Zo to meet me when I got out of prison. You were beginning to make a little time. You didn't want me back in Palmetto City. So you deposited forty-eight thousand dollars to my account in the National Bank of Habana."

"I did what?"

"You heard me. Beth was worth that much to you. Everything went fine until you learned that Beth had written me, offering to start all over."

Cliffton looked at Beth. "You did that?"

She pleated her handkerchief. "You know I did. I remember now. I told you. The morning I wrote it."

He nodded. "Yes. Now that you bring it up, I do recall you mentioned that you intended to write White."

I snuffed my cigarette. "You damn well remember. Because *Señor Peso* and Zo were the only two people who knew we were headed for that cabin. You followed us there. You were probably listening at the window when I read Beth's letter and told Zo we were through, that I was coming back to Palmetto City."

Cliffton shrugged. "Pure presumption on your part."

"You can prove where you were that night? You have an alibi?"

"This was what night?"

"Friday. Two nights ago."

Color crept into Cliffton's pale face. "No. I can't. At least I have no alibi I'd care to offer."

I continued. "You heard me read the letter. You heard what I said to Zo. And you saw another way out of your problem. It was you to whom Zo cried out just before you shot her and slugged me with that gaff hook. Maybe you meant to kill me. Maybe you didn't. It didn't make much difference one way or another. With me back in a cell at Raiford waiting to be burned for a murder I hadn't committed, I couldn't very well return to

111

Beth. And you are a patient man. You could wait. You knew that in time you would get what you wanted."

Cliffton was plenty nervous now. All three of us were. For different reasons. He picked up a cigarette from the table and dropped it. Instead of picking it up from the floor, he squashed it with the toe of his shoe. "You're not mentally right. You can't be. A jury would howl at that story."

I laid my last card on the table. "Okay. Let's test it. Let's all three go down to the station. I'll tell my story. You tell yours."

Cliffton shook his head. "No. I'm afraid we can't do that. I can't afford to. I'm a prominent man in Palmetto City and my business enemies would be certain to try to make capital of this."

Beth's voice was shrill. Shriller than I'd ever heard it. "You mean you're afraid the federal men might look at your invoices and begin to wonder where you're getting some of your goods that you'll be able to sell for less than your fellow merchants pay for it wholesale. It's been right in front of my nose all the time. And I didn't have sense enough to see it. No one but you could be *Señor Peso*.

The little man looked hurt. "You really believe that, Beth?"

"I do," she said, hotly.

"You think I'm that much of a heel?"

I said, coldly, "Any man who would rape another man's wife, force her against her consent, is capable of anything."

Cliffton looked from Beth to me. "Now I've raped someone. Who?"

I told him. "Beth."

He looked at Beth. She blushed and looked away.

It was a long time before he spoke. Then he said, quietly, "I see." He looked back at me. "Beth told you, eh?"

"She did."

"She told you where this attack took place?"

"In the cabin of your boat."

"When?"

"Six months ago." I brushed his excuse aside before he offered it. "Oh, I know what you're going to say. You were drunk. Beth told me that, too. That when you came to your senses you were as sorry as she that it had happened. That you begged her to divorce me and marry you."

Cliffton snuffed his cigarette. "I don't suppose it would do a bit of good to deny that I've ever had carnal knowledge of your wife, drunk or sober?"

I shook my head at him. "No. Naturally you'd deny it."

"Naturally," Beth said, shrilly.

112

"Naturally," Cliffton agreed.

We sounded like a bunch of goddamn parrots jabbering at each other. I was having all I could do to hold myself in. I was tired of being a gentleman. I wanted to pound on things and people. I wanted to smash my fists into faces. I wanted to get roaring drunk and forget the whole damn thing. But I couldn't. I had to keep my head. I had a date. Back at Raiford. With a chair. To pay for a life I hadn't taken. Zo's.

"I love you, Captain Charlie," she'd told me. While she was dying. Because some son of a bitch had killed her. Killed her in my arms.

Cliffton took another cigarette from his pack and lighted it with steady fingers. "So what happens now?"

I followed the instructions Beth had given me. "So now we walk out of here. Out to the car we have waiting in the drive."

"And then?"

"We drive down to the basin and your boat."

Cliffton repeated, "And then?"

"We'll take care of that when we get there," I told him.

Outside in the night again, I asked Beth if she could drive. She said she could. I rode in the back seat with Cliffton, both of us looking at the back of Beth's head. Her shoulder length bob fit her like a golden helmet. Hiding what thoughts? Only she could answer that.

Cliffton spoke only once during the ride. "What if we should happen to pass a police car and I should happen to cry out."

"I wouldn't if I were you," I advised him. "Believe me, Mr. Cliffton, I wouldn't."

A few minutes later we passed one. He had sense enough not to yell. Beth had never been a good driver. She hadn't improved. I rode with the feeling that I was on a balky merry-go-round that was gradually gathering momentum. If it went much faster, one of us was going to fly off into space.

The waterfront was dark and silent but here and there I could see a light in the cabin of a cruiser as the endless poker games and the caring for gear went on into the night. Matt Heely was still reading in the cabin of Cliffton's boat.

Beth parked the car a few boats down the mole.

"How did you get this far?" Cliffton asked me.

I told the truth. "God knows. I don't."

Beth got out of the car. She was breathing hard again. "All right. Take him out to the boat, Charlie."

I walked Cliffton down the mole with the gun in the small of his back. With my fingers crossed. Hoping we would not be

113

stopped. We weren't. His boat had a private pier. I walked him out on it slowly. Heely heard us coming. He put down the paper he was reading and opened the screen door into the cockpit. A lean, hatchet-faced cracker with gimlet eyes, he stood with one hand to his forehead trying to see into the dark, as a swift scudding cloud crossed the moon.

"Ahoy, the pier."

I could take Heely or leave him alone. A hard drinker with a penchant for jail bait and an uncanny ability to find an ace when he needed one, he wasn't popular along the water. On the other hand he was a good guide and a good seaman.

Beth was walking a few steps ahead of us. "It's Beth White, Captain Heely," she answered the hail.

"Oh," he said, quietly. "I see. Who's with you?"

"Joe Cliffton," Cliffton told him. "With a gun in my back."

Heely swung as if to re-enter the cabin.

I stopped him. "Hold it right there, Matt. Let's not have any unnecessary shooting. I'm the guy with the gun."

Heely froze, half in, half out of the cabin and shielded his eyes again. "That sounds like Charlie White."

I said, "It is."

He said, "Well, I'll be damned."

The tide was in. The cruiser was riding high. It wasn't much of a jump. Beth jumped down into the cockpit and as the moon floated out from behind the cloud, I caught a glimpse of white thigh, before she could paw down her skirt. "We want to talk to you, Captain," she told Heely. "But not here."

"Where then?" he puzzled.

"Out on the water," Beth said. "Slip your lines, turn your engine over and head out toward the island."

Heely looked at Cliffton. Cliffton looked down at the gun I was holding. "I guess you'd better do as you're told," he said. "It would seem that Beth and Charles White have some wild idea that I'm *Señor Peso.*"

"I've heard the name," Heely said.

He turned one engine over and put the screw in reverse to hold the big cruiser against the tide. ·

Beth asked, slightly breathless, "Has Lieutenant Gilly been here?"

Heely shook his head. "No, he ain't, Mis' White. There ain't been no police around. Not lately, anyway. Not since it was rumored along the water that Charlie was headed for Cuba."

The merry-go-round was moving faster now. It was all I could do to keep from using the gun to smack the smirk off his thin

114

face. I'd taken almost as much as I could, mentally, emotionally, physically. All I wanted was to get it over with. One way or another.

Cliffton asked if it was all right for him to sit in a deck chair. I said it was and sat in the chair beside him. Heely cast off the last line and walked back to his controls. There was a snortle in the water as the powerful screw took hold and eased the cruiser out of the slip. Clear of the slip and pier, Heely cut in his other engine and the big boat moved forward slowly, out into deep water, to the channel between the mainland and the island.

With deep water under him, Heely turned his head and looked at Cliffton again. "Now where?"

Cliffton's voice was crisp and bitter. "You'd better ask the Whites. It seems I haven't a thing to say."

"No. Not a thing," Beth said. Her breathlessness had left her. She seemed almost amused, but still a trifle frightened.

"Where?" Heely asked her.

She told him. "The island. Anchor in front of the house."

"Just as you say," he answered.

He gunned his engines a little and a tail of spray fanned out behind the cruiser.

Cliffton lighted a cigarette. "Were you out at the island this morning, Matt?"

Heely didn't bother to turn his head. "Why, yes. Come to think of it, I was."

Cliffton straightened in his chair. "What were you doing there?"

Heely turned and looked at him this time. "Why, as it so happens," he said, "I was taking a load of wetbacks off before the cops got to them. You ought to know. You told me to go get them and take them to the Springs."

"I knew it," Beth cried. "I knew it." Her fingers dug into my arm. "Would you swear that in court, Captain?"

Heely shook his head. "No. I'm not putting my neck into a federal noose for anyone. But I don't mind telling you folks. I been running stuff for Cliffton for some time. Ever since I smashed my boat. I'm walking the floor one night, see? Wondering which way to turn. And the phone rings. *'This is Señor Peso, Captain Heely,'* a guy tells me. *'How would you like to make some fast money?'* "

Beth exulted, "You hear that, Charlie? You hear what Matt just said?"

"Yeah,' I said. "I heard."

Cliffton stood up and walked to the rail. I stood up and walked

115

with him. But he wasn't trying to escape. All he wanted was some place to be sick.

I didn't blame the guy. I knew just how he felt.

CHAPTER TWENTY

THE MOON SLID out from behind a fast moving cloud and in behind another. In the brief flash of light Beth looked like an avenging angel. With yellow hair. And big breasts. And an overnight case in one hand. Clothes in it. She'd told me.

The moon came out and lighted her face again. It was contorted with anger, as she continued to beat the drum.

"There he is. The man who killed Zo and framed you for murder. The man who ruined our lives. The man who took four years of your life away from you. Because he wanted me."

I stood, unable to speak, the palm of my gun hand wet with sweat, having trouble breathing.

Beth looked at me, expectant. "Well, why don't you shoot him?"

I lifted the gun in my hand and looked from it to Cliffton. He stared back, his face white and haggard, but unafraid.

Beth continued to beat at me with her voice. "Well, go ahead. Don't just stand there. Shoot."

My throat was so contracted I had to squeeze the words out. Then they almost stuck in my mouth. "Yeah. But what happens then?"

Beth dropped her voice. "I told you, darling."

"Tell me again."

She might have been speaking to a slightly stupid child. "We take his body ashore and clear your name."

"How? By confessing to another murder?"

Beth stroked my arm. "But he's *Señor Peso*, Charlie. He killed Zo."

"How do we prove that if he's dead?"

"I'll show you. Just leave everything to me. Here. Let me have that gun."

116

I moved my gun hand away from her. "No. Why don't we take him ashore alive?"

"And have him lie out of it? You heard what Matt Heely said. He was willing to tell us but he wouldn't testify in court. Please let me have the gun."

I shook my head. "No dice. So Mr. Cliffton is *Señor Peso*. Why don't we take him ashore alive?"

Beth said, "Because—" and stopped there.

His back to the rail, Cliffton gripped it with both hands. "I can answer that," he said, quietly.

Heely had reached the far side of the channel and the narrow shelf in front of the old house. He reversed, then idled his engines and disappeared foreward along the narrow catwalk to drop his anchor. But not until he had made certain there were no small boats pulled up on shore. We were still standing as he had left us, when he dropped into the cockpit again. None of us saying anything. All of us busy with our thoughts. None of them pleasant.

Then the moon came out from behind a cloud and stayed out. Beth's face was screwed up as if she were crying, but no sound was coming out.

"I told you," Heely panted. "I told you over the phone it wouldn't work." He glanced apprehensively at the shore. "I was a goddam fool to let you talk me into this."

Beth made one last try. "But he—he *raped* me, Charlie."

I felt as sick as Cliffton had. "Yeah. So you told me. But then you told me so many things."

"You don't believe me?"

"No."

Cliffton's voice was sad. "I think I've known for some time. But then a man in love is a fool."

Heely spat the word. "Love. There ain't no such thing; it's all heat."

"I'm inclined to agree with you," Cliffton said.

I shook my head. "I'm not. I had a woman in love with me once. Her name was Zo."

Beth was breathing hard again. She gave me a dirty look and crossed the cockpit to Cliffton. "You do love me, don't you, Joe?"

The little man lighted a cigarette. "I suppose so. Having been in love with you for years, I don't suppose I'll ever be completely cured."

Beth rubbed her leg against his, like an amorous alley cat. On a back fence. Willing to rub more. "Then take me out of here.

117

Take me to Cuba. Anywhere. I don't dare go back to the mainland."

He said, "You're forgetting your husband."

Beth turned on me. "I hate him."

I didn't say anything.

Cliffton said, "Even so. He has the gun. Besides, what's this deal with Heely?"

"You can count me out," Heely said. "All I was interested in was the money."

"What was the deal?" I asked him.

He started to tell me, "After you'd killed Cliffton—"

Beth turned on him. "Shut up."

Heely shrugged and leaned against the screen door of the aft cabin.

Beth went back to work on Cliffton. "You must love me, Joe. You asked me to divorce Charlie and marry you a dozen times."

Cliffton said, "But that was before I 'raped' you."

Beth began to cry. "So I was desperate enough to lie. To try anything to get out of the scrape I'm in." Hysteria was creeping into her voice. "I'll make you a good wife. I'll do anything you ask, Joe. Anything."

I felt like I was running again. On through an endless nightmare. Only before, I'd been running toward Beth. Now I was running away from her. This was the woman I'd dreamed of for four years. This was the woman who had lain in my arms, her breath in my mouth, panting that she loved me.

I said, "I've been away for four years. I wouldn't have contested a divorce. Why didn't you divorce me and marry Mr. Cliffton while your chances were still good?"

"Damn you, Charlie White," Beth cursed me. "I wish I'd never met you."

The words sounded strange in her mouth.

"I can tell you that, White," Cliffton said. "Beth knew I wouldn't permit my wife to work and by that time she was in so deep that she didn't dare quit her job."

"So deep in what?"

"Running contraband through my store and writing checks for it to non-existent jobbers. Dummy concerns that she set up in Tampa, Orlando, St. Petersburg, Miami. Even as far away as Chicago and New York. Checks that she cashed herself. God knows how much she got away with. She was my confidential secretary. Her signature is as good as mine at any of a dozen banks that I can name."

Beth continued to cry silently.

118

Cliffton dropped his cigarette over the side. When it hit the water it made a small sound. Like a baby snake, just learning to hiss. "As to the night I 'raped' her, I think I can explain that. Even that long ago, the house of cards she'd built was beginning to get shaky. Twice federal men traced merchandise, believed to have been brought into the country without going through customs, to my store. But it was all supposition. Nothing could be proved." The little man sounded sad. "But Beth wanted a better hold on me than she had. She couldn't marry me. She didn't dare. So she tried to become my mistress. I still don't know why she didn't succeed. I'm just another guy. I like pretty women. I was with one the night this Cuban girl was killed. That's why I couldn't offer you an alibi."

Cliffton lighted a fresh cigarette and sucked smoke deep into his lungs. "But with Beth it was different. I'm a rich man, but a lonely one. I've spent all my life making money. Dreaming, some day, I'd meet the girl. I did. It was Beth. I knew it the first day she came to work for me. But then she was a married woman. I didn't dare say anything. Later, when I did, after you'd been sent away, she was already in so deep from stealing pennies, that she didn't dare try for the jackpot."

My right hand was tired holding the gun. I shifted it to my left hand. "But why this sudden urgency? Why should she want me to kill you now?"

He said, "The federal men are due at the store in the morning. And this time, they have me dead to rights. Over a matter of some perfume. And with our set-up at the store, it has to be myself or Beth. This time it so happens that I can prove I didn't place the order. I was in New York on a buying trip when it was introduced into our stock."

Beth stopped crying and felt in the bodice of her dress for a handkerchief.

"If she's lucky," Cliffton said, "she ought to get off with ten years. Possibly as little as five. On the other hand Uncle Sam doesn't like to be clipped. The judge may throw the book at her."

I asked, "And *Señor Peso—?*"

Cliffton shook his head. "There you have me. It's a cinch Beth was working with someone. And I'm almost positive it's not Heely. Matt isn't smart enough."

"Thank you," Heely said.

Beth had lost the handkerchief out of her bodice. She put the overnight case on the stool in front of the cockpit control and unsnapped the clasps.

119

Cliffton added, "I imagine the wetback business you mention was a last desperate attempt to make a final killing. I've heard they'll pay a thousand or more apiece to be brought into the country."

I said, "I've been offered as high as five."

Then something hit my hand. I felt the sting before the report. It sounded like someone had snapped his fingers, loud. I looked from my bleeding hand to the gun on the deck of the cockpit, then across the cockpit at Beth.

She was standing with her feet spread to steady herself against the roll of the cruiser, a small, black, ugly looking twenty-five caliber automatic in her hand. In the moonlight, her face was a series of flat white planes, all of them ugly.

"Pick up his gun," she told Heely.

Matt scuttled across the cockpit and scooped up the gun. "I was hoping you had one," he grinned "God knows I didn't." He leered at me. "But I have now."

"Like a pair of ducks," Cliffton breathed.

Beth's smile was as evil as her eyes. "Sitting ducks is the cliché," she corrected him. "Now I'll do some talking." Her eyes flicked over the side of the cruiser, across the shallows to the shore. "But not for long. What is there to say? Besides, *Señor Peso* is waiting for me. At the International Airport in Tampa. I trust."

Heely looked disappointed. "You'll never get away by plane."

Beth shrugged a slim white shoulder. "I don't intend to try. After we take care of Charlie and Mr. Cliffton, you're going to run me to Cuba."

Cliffton shook his head. "You'll never make it, Beth."

Her smile was superior. "Why not? Matt's cleared for his regular monthly trip to Cuba. And it won't make the least bit of difference to the Coast Guard if he starts a few hours early."

Heely looked toward Beth's breasts. "That's all right with me. That's fine. You have the money?"

Beth snapped the clasps on the overnight case. "I have." She looked at me. "And while we're on the subject of money, please give me that passbook, Charlie."

I tugged it from my hip pocket and handed it to her. "It's in my name. You can't collect it."

She put it between her breasts. "We'll see. You fool. I meant to go away with you, Charlie. I planned it that way. With you it wasn't pretense." Her smile was the twisted smile of every cheating wife in the world. "What's the matter? Didn't I please you? I tried so hard."

"Yes," I told her. "You did try. Too hard."

"And you didn't like your new wife?"

"Not enough to kill an innocent man for you."

"You knew," Beth accused.

"Not the first time," I admitted. "I thought maybe you really loved me. But I was pretty certain out at Sally's."

"How did you know?"

I told her. "You poured it on too thick. You tried too hard to be certain I was hooked."

"What did you know?"

"That everything you told me was a lie."

Beth squared her shoulders. "Light me a cigarette, Matt." Heely lighted one and handed it to her. "And now—?"

"Get your anchor up and get underway."

"And Charlie and Mr. Cliffton?"

"We'll take care of them as soon as we're underway."

"Right." Heely tucked the gun he was holding in the waistband of his pants, started to pull himself up on the catwalk to go forward and froze in fear, as Ken Gilly, his heavy service gun in hand, looked down from the flying bridge.

"Going somewhere?" Ken asked.

But he wasn't talking to Matt Heely. He was talking to Beth.

She turned slowly at his voice. Then she began to scream. One scream following another. Each one seeming to tear a fresh layer of membrane from her throat.

CHAPTER TWENTY-ONE

WHEN SHE COULD no longer scream, she panted, "You're at the airport in Tampa. Waiting for me. You have to be."

Ken had dropped into the cockpit by then. "You bitch," he named her. "You bitch." He was breathing as hard as she was. "You lying, two-timing bitch. You got me into this. And now you run out on me."

Heely went over the side. Ken didn't even see him go. He didn't know that Cliffton and I were pressed to the rail of the cockpit. Or didn't care. All he had eyes for was Beth.

He looked like a man who'd been through hell a long time. Tears streamed down his fat face, unnoticed.

" 'I love you, Ken,' you told me. 'If you'll do what I say we can both be rich.' That was four years ago. And like a fool I listened to you. I slept in my best friend's bed. I helped you send him to prison because you were afraid he might find out about us, find out there was no *Señor Peso* but you."

"Please, Ken," Beth begged him.

He slapped her with his free hand. "No. It's all torn now." He knew we were in the cockpit. "It doesn't matter what Charlie or Cliffton hear. They have a right to know. Everyone will know by morning. You're not going anywhere. I'm not going anywhere. We've been."

Beth attempted to distract him. "How did you get on this boat?"

"I've been on it since it left the basin. In the fore cabin. I knew by the tone of your voice that you were lying when you phoned me to meet you at the airport. And I figured you'd try to use Matt and leave me holding the bag."

Beth attempted to explain.

Ken cut her short. "I know. I heard. If you could chump Charlie into killing Cliffton, you figured you'd be in the clear, that you could stay in Palmetto City."

"That *we'd* be in the clear," Beth panted.

Ken shook his head. "No. I never figured with you. Except as a willing stooge. A stooge you paid off with your body. And the fat cracker boy loved it. Loved it because he loved you. Because he's always loved you." Ken glanced at me briefly. "What did she tell you, Charlie? I mean about us."

I said, "That you, well, got together one night, shortly after I was sent away. And from then on, you forced your attentions on her, threatening to kill her when she tried to stop seeing you."

Ken continued to cry, great dry sobs racking his body. Did you ever see a man cry? A strong man? It's not nice. His tears weren't coming from tear ducts. They were being pumped out of his heart.

"I imagined it was something like that," he said. "But that wasn't the way it happened. It started long before you were sent away. I was the guy who called you on the phone." It was the voice I'd heard for four years, lying awake nights in my cell, staring up into the darkness. *"This is Señor Peso, Captain White. How would you like to make two thousand dollars?"*

I couldn't help it. I gasped, "You son of a bitch."

"I'm all of that," Ken nodded. "But all I ever was, was a voice. A voice on the phone. Except one time."

"And that one time?"

Ken wiped his fat cheeks with the back of his free hand. "Was last Friday on Dead Man's Bay."

"It was you who killed Zo?"

He nodded. "That's right. I also tried to kill you. I thought I had."

"Why?"

"Because even then I knew that we'd played out our string, that time was running out on us." His fat face was a mask of tragedy. "And Beth was running out on me. I had Matt locate Zo on his last trip to Habana and advance her money to meet you. I arranged for a boat to pick you up and take you down to Cuba. The money was Beth's idea. She said the figures in a bankbook would make it look good. Then I learned that the figures were real. I learned she had written you and that she had sent you money to come to her."

"And if I didn't come to Palmetto City?"

"She planned to join you in Habana, cut out Zo, at least long enough to recover the money. The forty-eight grand was insurance. Oh, Beth was smart. She thought of everything. She covered every angle. But me. So I drove up to Dead Man's Bay and did what I had to do to make certain that you didn't come back, but you did. And somehow I'm not sorry. I'm glad that it's over."

Beth brushed her arm against his. "Don't talk like that, Ken. We still have a chance together."

He shook his head at her. "No. We had our chance."

She pressed even closer to him. "Don't talk like that."

Ken used his free hand to push her away from him. Gently. "No. It's gone. The boat's sailed. It sailed when you went to bed with Charlie. To find out how much he knew, to tuck him away as an ace. To use against me. In case I stepped out of line. But you almost slipped up there. When you sent him out to the island to hide. You forgot we hadn't had time to move the wet-backs in the attic. They almost killed Charlie. Then Matt got them off barely in time."

He glanced at me again, briefly. "You were in the swamp, weren't you, Charlie?"

"I was."

"I knew. I tried to kill you. I wanted to kill you, then."

"And now?"

Ken looked at me again, longer this time. "I've done enough to you, fellow. Don't you think?"

I didn't say anything. What was there to say? Besides, he had a gun. All I had were my fists.

Ken continued, "Then, tonight out at Sally's tore it."

Beth stared in fear. "What do you know about Sally's? How do you know?"

Ken looked at her dull-eyed. "How does anyone know about anything along the water? I know you met Charlie in room seven. I know you were there an hour. There was only one thing you, being you, could be doing. You were paying him in advance for something you wanted him to do. Something clever that you'd schemed up in that pretty little head of yours."

Beth backed away as far from him as she could. "No. Don't look at me that way, Ken."

"How do you want me to look at you?"

Beth wet her dry lips with her tongue. "I'll go away with you now. We'll go away together." She picked up the overnight case. "Look. I have most of the money."

Ken slapped it out of her hand. "I've never been too interested in the money angle. You know that. All I wanted was you."

Beth pleaded with him. "And you can have me, Ken." She repeated, "I'll go away with you. We'll go away together."

"Where?"

"Anywhere you want to go."

"How?"

"On this boat."

"I can't run it and neither can you."

"By plane then. We'll go to the airport in Tampa."

Ken gestured out at the water. "And how do we get through that?"

Beth's eyes followed the gesture and her face screwed up again as if she were going to scream. The channel immediately offshore looked like a Christmas tree, hung with the red and green running lights of cruisers, half-cabins, power-boats.

There was a Coast Guard boat with the cocky young j.g. silhouetted against the moonlight.

"Ahoy, the cruiser," he called.

Beth screamed at me. "You did that. You didn't intend to go through with what you promised from the start. That's what you and Frenchy were whispering about. You warned him to alert the harbor."

"That's right," I answered.

She lifted her shoulder length yellow hair up and away from

the back of her neck. "I won't be arrested. I won't." Then she realized she still had the small gun in her hand and pointed it at me. "Run this boat out of here, fast."

I shook my head at her. "I can't."

"Why not?"

"The hook's down. Remember? Matt was just going forward to lift it when Ken joined the party."

The j.g.'s voice was sharper this time. "Ahoy, the cruiser. Who's aboard?"

Cliffton spoke for the first time. "Cliffton, lieutenant," he called. "And I'd appreciate it if you'd board us. We're in a little trouble."

Beth emptied the small gun at him. "No!"

Lead smacked into the side of the cockpit, screaming off the metal it touched. Then, sobbing as if her heart were broken, Beth raced the few feet to the stern and a white thigh showed to her hip, as she straddled the wide fish box. "I won't be arrested. I won't."

"No, Beth," Ken said quietly. "Don't try it."

She ignored him and slithered over the stern, cursing as her dress caught on the raised metal burgee socket. There was a sound of tearing cloth. Then a splash. Then she was scrambling up on the shelf and stumbling across it toward shore. A big spotlight on the Coast Guard boat came on and pinned the scene against the night.

Beth's dress and slip were gone. She raced on, her blonde hair trailing behind her. Looking like the beautiful but evil creature that she was. Released from the hell of her own making.

"No," Ken panted beside me. "Not that."

His gun bucketed in my ear. I tried to knock up his arm, too late. A red stain appeared on Beth's white back, just under her left shoulder blade. She took another uncertain step or two and fell face forward into the water and there was another splash as Ken went over the side and floundered through the shallows to her, his fat shoulders shaking again, calling softly, "Beth, darling, sweetheart."

Sergeant Strawn met him wading back, with Beth's white body in his arms, tears streaming down his fat face. I stood dry-eyed, watching. It was his right to carry her. She was his dead, not mine.

As they met, Ken held out his service revolver. "It's all right, Bill," he said. "I won't give you any trouble." He held Beth's body closer. "We won't give you any trouble any more. . . ."

It was dawn when they let me leave the station. There wasn't much I could tell them. I told them what little I could. With the exception of the hood in the old house. Ken admitted that he'd hired the hood to kill me. Strawn said they would question me again later. I didn't see any sense in confessing something that couldn't be traced to me. I'd had all of cells that I wanted.

Cliffton and I walked down the worn steps together. He looked tired and old, much older than he had. The hunt for the killer was over. I'd been found and I wasn't wanted. But in dying, the way she had, Beth had killed a little something in all of us.

In forcing him to do what he'd done, she'd killed Ken outright. Something in Cliffton died. He would always be lonely now. I knew that I would be. But not for Beth. My love had died on Dead Man's Bay.

We stood in front of the station a moment, trying to find something to say to each other. There didn't seem to be anything.

"Well," Cliffton said, finally, "I'll see you around, White."

I said, "Yeah. Sure thing, Mr. Cliffton.'

I watched him walk away, uptown toward his store. Then I walked slowly toward the water. Frenchy was waiting for me on the curb. He fell in step with me but didn't say anything.

I walked on, thinking of Swede. He'd been right. And he'd been wrong. Beth and Ken had swum out of the school. And look what happened to them. But on the other hand he'd called Zo a fancy dame. And it hadn't been like that at all. Zo had loved me. She'd died telling me so. I'd done the same things with her as I had with Beth. But there was a difference somehow. It wasn't just a matter of making love to a man that made a woman good or bad. Zo had probably had a lot more men than Beth. But Zo had known. She'd warned me. Zo had told me:

"This woman does not love you. I am a woman. I know."

Zo had been right. It made it difficult for a man. I hadn't known what to think or what to do. What was right? What was wrong? Which was the real? Which was the false?

At the edge of the basin, Frenchy stopped to roll a cigarette. "You got any dough, Charlie?" he asked me.

I shook my head. "No. I haven't got a dime."

He licked and lighted his cigarette. "Neither have I. But you're welcome to bunk on the boat as long as you care to, Charlie. I can always scrape up a meal and a bottle. And we can even fish partners again, if you want."

"I'd like that, Frenchy," I said. And borrowed his makings. I

126

walked on with him to the battered half-cabin in the basin.

But long after he'd turned in, I sat on the live bait well. Smoking. Listening to the drip of the condensation off the roof of the cabin tinkle in the silence. Taking a drink from time to time. Looking out at the undulating water taking on color from the sun. The past was dead. There was no use thinking about it. But the rising sun, shining on the water, gave me hope. Perhaps, somewhere out there beyond the horizon, there was another Zo. Waiting for me.

I hoped so.

www.ingramcontent.com/pod-product-compliance
Lightning Source LLC
Chambersburg PA
CBHW020147180626
46810CB00004B/1772